The Illest Taboo

(An Enemies to Lovers Romance)

by

K.L. Hall

D1400554

This book is a work of fiction. Names, characters, places and incidents are either the product of the author's imagination or are used fictionally. Any resemblance to actual persons, living or dead, or to actual events or locales is entirely coincidental.

This e-book is licensed for your personal enjoyment only. This e-book may not be re-sold or given away to other people. If you like to share this book with another person, please purchase an additional copy for each person you share it with.

Copyright © 2021 K.L. Hall. All rights reserved. Including the right to reproduce this book or portions thereof, in any form. No part of this text may be reproduced in any form without the express written permission of the author.

the illest taboo synopsis.

Between student loans, an unexpected rent hike, and a career that has her living paycheck to paycheck, 24-year-old River Newman is swimming in her share of debt. She longs for the lavish lifestyle of her best friend, Suki. From the matching his and her Maserati's she and her husband Luca roll in, to the iced-out diamond ring Suki lugs around on her ring finger, they are serious #couplegoals. Yet, their most prized possession is their five-year-old daughter, and River's goddaughter, Noemi. Just days away from eviction, River is hit with the tragic news that both Suki and Luca were killed in a car accident, leaving her to raise Noemi as her own. There's only one thing standing in her way, Luca's brother, Maverick. Not only is he Noemi's last living blood relative, he's also the type of man River avoids.

Maverick Muhammad Malone is fresh off a five-year bid and determined to turn his life around. After becoming a licensed tattoo artist while incarcerated, he plans to put all the money he made as the spearhead of East Atlanta's most sought-after drug ring into a legitimate tattoo business and leave the mess of his past behind. After learning of his brother's death, he quickly finds himself being dragged back into the lion's den. When Noemi is temporarily placed in his custody, he knows he's not equipped to take on the role of fatherhood alone. He enlists the help of the one person who knows her best, River.

When Maverick offers her an opportunity to become Noemi's live-in nanny, rent-free, she sees it as an opportunity to save her favorite little girl from a life in the system and herself from her financial woes. But will she be able to put her judgments aside and agree to live under the same roof as the man she's despised for years? With a pending court hearing looming over him, the stakes are higher than ever. Maverick will have to prove that he's capable of keeping his hands clean, while secretly planning to avenge his brother's death. For these two, falling in love was never a part of the plan, but if they can save the child, they just may end up saving each other too.

epigraph.

"He said, enter at your own risk.
I am not responsible for the misery I will bring you.
It's just a matter of time before I start to destroy you.
Let me warn you.

I've dealt with worse boy.
Let's see who breaks who first.
It won't be my first time."

Elaine- "Risky"

Prologue

February 7, 2016

River Newman

It was Superbowl Sunday. The Panthers were playing the Broncos, and I was spending the evening with my best friend, Suki, her man Luca and his brother, Maverick. With my laptop nestled in between my crisscrossed legs, I typed away at my research paper that was due at midnight. I didn't come up for air until I'd entered in my last citation and submitted it. That's when I realized I'd been left all alone in the living room. After closing my laptop, I made my way into the kitchen to eat my fill of pizza and wings. Walking past the laundry room, I overhead Suki mumbling, followed by an even deeper mumble. My stroll slowed down, and I was able to hear the conversation more clearly.

"He doesn't have to know," Maverick told her.

"I agree, he doesn't," Suki replied, "at least not right

now."

There was a pause followed by a loud sigh. "Good."

"I'd be lying if I said I didn't miss you," she told him. "You know what you do to me, Mav. You fuckin' drive me crazy. I can't stop thinkin' about the night we spent, and—"

Before I could hear his response, Luca's voice rang out from around the corner. I spun around and pressed my back against the laundry room door. "Yo, River. Where everybody at?"

"Huh? Oh, I uh, I don't know. I think maybe Mav went out to his car, and I think maybe Suki is upstairs?"

"That nigga not outside. I just got back to the house. Suki sent me out for some shit she needed for her hamburger dip."

I glanced down at the two plastic bags in his grasp. "Oh, okay. I just finished my paper, so I don't know—uh, why don't you go find him, and I'll find her?"

He put the bags down on the counter and nodded. "Yeah, aight."

"Okay." I nodded. Heart pounding a million beats per second, I turned toward the door and gently knocked. "He's looking for you...both of you," I said against the door before walking away.

    With a freshly poured glass of white wine in my hand, I watched them both walk out of the laundry room, one a few minutes after the other as if no one would notice. I scoffed. Suki and Luca had only been dating for a few months when she found out she was pregnant. Instead of leaving her to fend for herself or toss her a few hundred dollars to make it all go away, he stayed. Not only did he stay, but he also moved her into his home and made it clear to everyone within the Atlanta city limits that she was his. Everything between them had happened too fast, and it became clear to me that Luca deserved better. How either of them could betray a good man like that was beyond me. Mav's eyes locked with mine, and I quickly rolled them. Without saying a word to each other, he pressed his phone to his ear and headed out to find his brother. Suki walked over to me with a sour look on her face.

    "What all did you hear?" she asked.

    "Enough," I told her.

    Suki huffed before pushing her hair behind her ears. "Look, it's not what it looks like, okay?"

    "Then what does it look like?" I asked, folding my arms across my chest. "Because you and I both know whatever is going on between you two doesn't need to be going on."

"Nothing is going on, okay? I put a stop to it. I'm with Luca and that's all that matters. He knows that."

"But does he respect it? Better yet, do you?" I quizzed, letting my judgements fly.

Suki sucked her teeth. "Listen to me," she said, grabbing my shoulders, "nothing is going on between us. I told him that it needed to end, and he agreed. End of story, River. Okay?"

I nodded while throwing up my hands. "It's your life, girl. Live it how you wanna," I told her.

"Thank you," she said, running her hand down her pregnant belly. "I love Luca, okay? I do. Me, him, and this baby are going to be a family."

I shrugged. "You don't have to prove anything to me, Su."

She lifted her chin before turning her attention to my wine glass. "You're lucky you get to drink."

"It's not like you can't drink forever, just another few months, right?"

Suki nodded. "Yeah, unless this little one wants to come early. You know due dates are never one hundred percent—at least that's what my doctor told me."

I pressed my lips tightly together. "Right."

I no longer wanted to have the conversation we were having. Suki had always had it all; the looks, the body, and the desire to get whatever and whoever she wanted. From her striking honey brown eyes to her slim-thick physique and naturally long hair, Suki could easily be the apple of any man's eye. It wasn't a complete shock that she'd obviously captured the attention of both the Malone brothers, I just hoped she knew how to treat the burn she'd acquire from playing with fire.

"Anyway, let me start working on this hamburger dip before Luca has a heart attack."

"Yeah, I'll let you get to that. I'm gonna go chill out and catch the rest of the game."

"You actually enjoy watching the game?" she asked.

I gave a half shrug. "Not really, but something about seeing a bunch of sweaty men running up and down the field makes me feel all warm and tingly inside," I said, hoping to lighten the mood.

Suki chuckled. "You're so weird, River."

"Love you too." I smiled.

Before I could exit the kitchen, Luca approached me. "Yo ladies, can I get y'all to step outside for me?"

"Outside? Baby, it's literally winter," Suki attested.

"It'll be quick, I just want to show you something."

"I'll grab both of our coats," I told her.

We stepped out onto the balcony to see an oversized tent swallowing up the middle of the backyard.

"Oh my God, baby! What's the occasion?" she squealed while putting her hands over her mouth in total surprise.

"It's for you. C'mon, let's go inside."

I followed behind Suki and Luca as we made our way inside. I smiled, feeling the warmth of the heated tent against my face. My eyes lit up at the sight of a complete winter wonderland. The first thing I noticed was the string quartet playing their rendition of John Legend's *Ordinary People* in the middle of the custom-built ice-skating rink in the middle of the tent.

"Baby, oh my God! All this for me? Why? And how did I not even notice any of this was going on outside?"

"I have my ways."

Suki squealed and threw her arms around him. "It's so beautiful in here!"

I nodded as my eyes took in the snow-white curtains draping the walls from the ceiling to the floor with royal blue and white light effects to really set it off right.

Oversized white glittered Manzanita trees with acrylic chains dripping off them lined the perimeter of the rink, as snowflakes and crystals hung from the ceiling. I knew money was no object to Luca, but I could only hope he had a bigger plan behind his grand gesture and not just because it was the Superbowl.

"Wow! This is so beautiful. I feel like the third wheel, so I'm going to let you two enjoy the rest of your night. I'll see myself out."

"Nah, wait up a second, River. I want you to be here for what happens next."

"And what's that?" I asked.

Luca turned his attention back to Suki and grabbed her hand. They two of them made their way closer to the quartet who began to play KC and Jo-Jo's *All My Life*.

"Oh shit," I muttered underneath my breath.

"The fuck is he doing?" Maverick asked, stepping up behind me.

"Shh! I think he's about to propose," I whispered.

"Fuckin' fool," he muttered.

My eyebrows knitted as heat burned my cheeks. How could he stand there and hate on his own flesh and blood at a pivotal milestone in his adult life?

"I think it's sweet."

He sucked his teeth. "You would."

As much as I wanted to rip into him and tell him that he wasn't shit, I heard Luca speak up and asked the question that my ears were burning to hear. "Suki Diamond Lawrence, will you marry me?"

"Yes! Oh my God, yes! I love you, baby!"

Luca slid the glacier of a diamond ring onto her finger before pulling her into his arms. "I love you too."

Five Years Later

River Newman

My body jarred in between my bedsheets as my eyes popped open. I groaned before rolling over to shut off my first of four alarms. By the third one, I'd managed to reach my hand over to the other side of the bed to feel around for my boyfriend, Leander. Instead, I felt cold sheets crumpled into the comforter. I rolled over and opened my eyes to verify what my hands had already known to be true. Leander was gone.

The fourth alarm went off, and I swiped my phone to silence it before calling him.

"Yeah, hello?" he answered on the fourth ring.

"Hello? Baby, where are you? I woke up and you weren't here. You know I don't like it when you leave without saying goodbye," I whined, trying to shake the sleep from my voice.

"Didn't you read my text?" he asked, with not an ounce of warmth in his tone.

"Your text? What text? I just woke up and saw you weren't here, so I called you. What'd it say?"

"Just read the text, River. I—I gotta go."

He ended the call, and I immediately frowned before checking my messages.

Bae [5:42am]: River, I know you've noticed the distance I've been putting between us for a while now. Just to end the suspense, I took a job in Chicago, and I didn't know how to tell you. You've been a great girlfriend, but right now, I just think it's better for both of us to be single and go down our own paths. I hope one day you can forgive me.

Furious, I screamed and immediately dialed him back.

"Your call has been forwarded to an automatic voice message system. 4-0-4-5-5-5-1-1-1-1 is not available. Please record your message after the beep."

14

"Oh, this mothafucka has got to be kidding me!"

BEEP

"Leander! Are you kidding me right now? This is how you do me, nigga? After almost three years! THIS is how you treat ME? Call me back now!"

BEEP

"Leander! Your ass better be on that fuckin' plane or something for not answering my calls or calling me back! You can't just say what you said and think I'm just going to let it go. What about how I feel, huh? Call me back as soon as you land!"

BEEP

"You must really think you can play me by not calling me back! You know what, fuck you, Leander! Fuck you! Fuck your family! Fuck your fuckin' plane! I hope that shit crash and you the only mothafucka on the plane that die!"

BEEP

(Sigh) "You know what, I took it too far. That was too far. I'm sorry. You know I would never want anything to happen to you. It's just—how could you do me like this? Leave without giving me any explanation? Am I not worth even that much to you? Please, baby…just call me back."

BEEP

"Leander, this is the last time I'm calling you. I just need to hear your voice and know that you're okay and if you don't want to talk right now, I'll accept that. Just know that I'm here whenever you're ready, and I—I love you."

After that last message, I switched from bearing my feelings over his voicemail to turning my attention to his text messages. Every text I sent just ended up being floating message bubbles without the "delivered" receipt underneath. My consecutive Facetime calls rang with no answer. I even tried to reach out to him on Facebook and he'd blocked me, couldn't even find his profile.

It was like he was single handedly trying to erase the last two and a half years of his life as if I never existed. If I didn't get up in the next four minutes, I was sure to be late for work. So, I peeled myself out of bed with my broken heart weighing a ton.

With tears in my eyes, I whipped my Hyundai Elantra into the first parking space I could find. My shoulder hurriedly brushed past the "Home of the Lions" banner right outside the entrance of the school. I only had three minutes to spare before I was considered late. I'd been working as a second-grade teacher at Willowdale Elementary for three years and struggling to make ends meet.

Shuffling down the hallway, I tapped my nails against the email icon on my phone and opened an unread email from my landlord. My forehead creased as I soaked in the news about an unexpected rent hike, making my rent two hundred dollars higher. Even with Leander's extra income, I could barely afford my half of that plus all of the other bills I was paying.

"Fuck," I mumbled as I rested my back against the aged couch in the teacher's lounge. For a second, I'd forgotten that Leander had jumped ship. His lack of extra income was going to hurt any chance I ever had at saving any money. With him at the forefront of my mind once again, I tapped his name and pressed the phone to my ear while swiping a leftover cookie from Teacher Appreciation Week off the table and biting into it. My lips twisted at the stale taste. I tossed it along with the rest of them in the overflowing trash can.

"Your call has been forwarded to an

17

automatic voice—"

"Good morning, Miss Newman," Principal Jones said before walking over to the copy machine.

"Morning," I muttered with a nod.

I promptly turned my eyes back to the microwave while it heated my instant oatmeal. Seconds later, he spoke up again.

"So, you got plans for the summer?"

"Nope, you?" I asked over the beeping of the microwave.

"Ah, the family and I always drive to Florida and spend a week there seeing family, hitting the beach, you know."

"Sounds fun," I told him, forcing a smile.

As much as I knew I needed to put my game face on, I was having a hard time swimming from the depths of my feelings. For the past two and a half years, I'd been someone's woman. Two hours prior, I was happy in love. Now, I'd been reduced to no calls, texts, or Facetime like a bad one-night stand. There was no way I could easily wrap my head around that. The last words he wrote me hung on my mind like grapes on a vine.

"Well, if I don't get a chance to tell you before the end of the school year in a few weeks, have a great summer,

18

and we'll see you back next year," Principal Jones said, jarring me back to reality.

I nodded. "Yeah, you too."

"Thanks!"

"Oh, uh—before you go, did you get a chance to read my email? I sent it a couple days ago and haven't heard anything back yet."

"I apologize. I haven't gotten around to it. What was it about?"

"I was asking to get on your schedule some time this week to discuss a few of my students."

"Er—today's not good but let me take a look at it when I get back to my office, and we'll make time to talk after school tomorrow. Sound good?"

"Yes, sir, thank you."

"No problem. Have a good day," he said, before taking a sip from his coffee cup.

"Thanks, same to you."

I shoved my phone inside my purse and gathered up my things to head to my classroom. School hadn't even begun, and I could already predict that I'd have a hurricane-sized headache before the day was over.

TWO

River

I'd managed to make it to the weekend with only an ounce of my sanity left. As much as I wanted to eat my weight in Ben & Jerry's ice cream and sit in the dark and watch *Waiting to Exhale* on repeat, I had to pull myself out of my sorrows to attend my goddaughter, Noemi's, fifth birthday party. As my car whizzed up their long driveway, I started to realize just how fast the past five years had really flown by. I would never understand how years changed from one to the next in the blink of an eye, but the days inched by at a snail's pace. I let out one oversized sigh before checking my reflection in my rearview mirror and flipped through the rolodex of my mind in search of something to smile about. At least the oversized light-wash mom jeans I had on would allow me to eat my woes in overly sweet icing and other pound-packing delights.

I swiped the pastel pink envelope off the passenger seat before swinging my legs out of the car and letting my worn chucks hit the pavement. After making my way through the maze of cars to the front door, I rang the doorbell and decided to call Leander one more time while I waited. To no surprise, it still went straight to voicemail. Frustrated, I ran my palm down my lace bustier and then shoved it in the pocket of my black leather jacket.

Suki swung the enormous front door open wearing a pink chiffon two-piece skirt set with a pair of cat eye sunglasses over her eyes. She was giving off modern day *Clueless* vibes. "It's about time you got here, Ri!"

I smacked my teeth. "Now you know I wouldn't miss this."

"You better not have because I'm so over these gossipin' ass mothers! These bitches make me wanna take a shot or three!"

I put on a smile. "You know me, River to the rescue."

She pulled me into her arms. "C'mon, I want you to see the amazingness that is outside! I truly outdid myself this time."

I followed behind her as her four-inch stiletto heels click-clacked against the polished wooden floor. One of Suki's favorite pastimes was showing off, so I already knew the party was going to be fancy as fuck for no reason. They were beyond tying balloons to a mailbox and taping up a few streamers. All of Noemi's birthday parties looked like

21

they'd come from a page ripped straight out of the Kardashians' book, and her fifth was no different. As soon as we stepped outside, I could see that almost every square inch of their backyard had been decked out. From the custom balloon arch spelling out Noemi's name, to the chocolate ice cream fountain, and the unicorn-shaped inflated bounce house, extravagant was an understatement.

"Damn girl, y'all went all out, didn't you?" I asked, adding my card amongst the dozens of gift bags sprouting with an array of neon and pastel colored tissue paper on the gift table.

Suki shrugged. "Yeah, girl. She thinks she's a unicorn, so we gave her unicorns. Plus, you know Noemi is the fuckin' apple of Luca's eye. Whatever she wants, she gets."

"And so do you."

"I know." She smiled, playing with the silky tendrils of her hair.

"All I'm sayin' is, how much did all of this cost and why have you never thrown me such an elaborate bash as this?"

"Because I didn't push your big-headed ass out of my cooch." She laughed. "But no, this year, you and I are going on a girls trip. All expenses paid!"

"I mean, I do have a birthday coming up, and I could really use the getaway," I admitted.

"Say no more!"

"So, where we going?" I asked, feeling myself light up for the first time in days.

"Hmm, somewhere sexy, you know? We can't go nowhere basic that any fuckin' body can go to. I'm thinking...the Maldives or St. Barts. Yeah, St. Barts, it's settled!"

I shrugged lazily. "I don't even know where that is."

"It doesn't matter because we're going! We'll book the tickets tomorrow!"

"Wait, are you serious?"

"Yes! You're my best friend!" she said, hooking her arm in mine.

"Luca is gon' be fine with you whisking me off on an expensive girl's trip?"

"Girl, please. The pussy is the key to everything. Plus, if he ever had a problem with it, I've got my own money. Trust, I can afford it."

My forehead creased. "Since when did you start working?" I asked, shocked at the news that my best friend had actually gone out and got a job.

"Don't try to play me, bitch! I make things happen when I need to make things happen, aight? A bitch is always thinkin' about her next move."

"Well, I'm proud of you!"

She flashed a wide smile. "Thank you! Give a bitch some props when props are due."

"You right, you right. My bad!" I said, bumping my hip against hers.

"Wait a minute, where's your man at?"

"Uh," I breathed, slow to reveal my recent break up. "He's, you know, at work. Work stuff, yeah. So, he couldn't make it."

She shot up a questioning eyebrow at me, and I darted my eyes over to Noemi's uncut five-layer birthday cake to shield myself from her judgment. Instead of pressing me harder, she took the conversation in another direction.

"I can't believe my little baby is five, Ri."

"I swear, I was just thinking about that in the car. Where did the time go?"

She nodded. "It went by fast, didn't it?"

"Too fast. Next thing you know, you'll have a sassy teenager on your hands."

"Trust me, girl. That one is already giving me all the sass I can handle. A bitch can't take no more."

We both chuckled. "What do you expect? She's just like you. Where is she at anyway?"

"Uh," she said, eyes scanning the yard. "There she is, right over by the DJ booth dancing with some of her little friends."

"I'm gonna go say hi."

"Ugh, fine, but make it quick. I don't want any of these boring ass wives coming over to me trying to make conversation."

I chuckled. "Girl, what is your beef?"

She rolled her eyes. "It's bad enough they had to be invited because of, you know, the business—but just because they're here, doesn't mean I have to interact with they asses. You know how antisocial I am."

"That I do know." I nodded. "I'll be right back."

On my way over to Noemi, I made a sidebar over to the buffet and piled my plate high with all things unicorns—including cookies, dessert kababs, and donuts. "This is what dreams are made of," I mumbled to myself before biting into a glittery cream-filled treat.

"Hey there, birthday girl!" I said, walking up to Noemi, who was dripping in glitter from head to toe. One look at Noemi and it wasn't hard to tell which side had the more dominant genes. She was Suki's mini-me.

Her face lit up and she threw her arms open to hug me. "Auntie!"

I sat on one of the fluffy stools and pulled her onto my lap. "Happy birthday to Auntie's favorite girl!"

"Thank you!"

"What did you get for your birthday?"

"Um, well—I don't know everything yet, but I did get three new cars!"

I gasped. "Three?"

The corners of her mouth curled upwards into a smile. "Yeah."

"Can I have one? I need a new car!"

She broke into a short laugh. "No, but you can ride with me."

"Which one we gon' ride in first?"

"Umm…"

"C'mon, tell me! The suspense is killing me!" I squealed, while reaching out to tickle her.

She squirmed and giggled in my grasp. "The one like Mommy!" She screeched, referring to the winter white Mercedes G-class her mother whipped around in.

"Ohhhh, I can't wait! That's going to be so much fun!"

"OH SHIT! LOOK WHO THE FUCK IS HOME? BREAK OUT THE GOOD SHIT!" Luca roared across the party.

Before my eyes could follow the sound, Noemi spoke up. "Who's that man Daddy's talking to?" she asked.

I followed her eyes to see Luca and his brother, Maverick, embracing beside the cotton candy vendor. "Oh shit," I mumbled.

"Aww! You said a bad word!"

I quickly slapped my hand over my mouth and frowned. "Auntie is sorry! Look, you go dance with your friends. I'm going to go find your mommy, okay?"

Noemi nodded before zooming away. Without trying to make it look like I was being nosey, I let my eyes slowly scan the party. One look at Suki, and I could tell her mind was spinning. Maverick had been incarcerated for the past

27

five years. He'd missed their wedding and the birth of his one and only niece. Out of the blue, he'd reappeared, and we were all shook at his surprising return. The moment I was within arm's reach of Suki, I whipped my gaze back to Maverick. Looking at him made my fuckin' skin crawl. It wasn't until he looked back at me that I realized I'd had my eyes locked on him for too long. *Fuck, I've been spotted.* His mouth twisted into a smirk, telling me he noticed me noticing him. I quickly turned my attention to Suki, searching for the truth in her eyes.

"It's over, right?"

A second passed, then another. "What? Yes, River. Of course it is. Why would you even bring that up?"

"I'm sorry, it's just the look in your eyes, it's telling…"

She sucked her teeth. "The only thing it's telling is that I'm surprised he's here. I—I didn't know he was getting out, nor did I know he would show up here, today of all days. I mean look around, Ri. All eyes are on him."

My eyes retraced their path to him, this time taking him in a little more. I found comfort in knowing my prying eyes weren't alone. He stood there, cradling a champagne flute in his large hands. His skin was an almond, caramel swirl mashup—even from ten feet away it looked as soft as butter. His simple crisp white t-shirt clung to his muscles as if it had been painted on. Tattoo ink drizzled down his arms all the way to his iced-out wrists. Camouflaged pants and two gold chains around his neck completed his ensemble. He smiled and *everything stopped.* The Black and West Indian blood pumping through his veins made everything about him command respect. Even the elements of space and time bent to his will. He was a free man with a point to prove, and he had the fresh cut to prove it.

"He looks…damn good though," she said, stealing glances at him through her sunglasses.

Why the fuck did he have to get out? I thought to myself. Suki and Luca had become the epitome of couple goals since they tied the knot. He was her protector, and she was his peace. Maverick was nothing but an unnecessary distraction. I could only pray Suki meant what she said.

"I guess, I should go speak and introduce him to his niece. His ass better not have shown up empty handed either."

I scoffed. "Mmk. I'm going to run inside and go to the bathroom."

"Okay, we'll be cutting the cake soon and singing *Happy Birthday*, so don't miss it."

"Sure thing," I said over my shoulder.

With a crumbled piece of paper towel in hand, I made my way out of the bathroom and headed toward the door to go back outside. The instant my hand reached out for the knob, the door turned, landing me face to face with the only person at the party I didn't want to cross paths with.

He flashed a smile at me. "River?"

I nodded. "Guilty."

"It's been a minute. A nigga can't get a welcome home greeting?"

"Time really does fly when you don't give a fuck, but uh—welcome back," I said, unable to hide the bitterness in my tone.

I didn't know him or Luca from Adam before Suki started dating his brother. But I heard what I heard loud and clear, and I wasn't a fan. As much as I wanted to tell him about himself, I'd save it for another day.

"Damn, it's like that?"

The deepness of his voice vibrated my nerves. "It's been like that."

"What's your beef?" he asked, his russet brown eyes peering down at me.

"We don't speak, Mav. We never really have. I don't know why you're even talkin' to me right now."

"Damn, shawty you sound uptight. If you need a nigga to handle that lemme know."

I scoffed. He had some nerve. "Oh please," I said while rolling my eyes as hard as I could. "You've probably been swimming in an oasis of hoes the moment you stepped outside the prison walls. Besides, my man handles all of this *very* well."

"Oh, you got a man? My fault, my fault," he said, tossing up his surrendering hands.

His ego was so visible, I could almost watch it grow in real time. I needed to make it clear that I was off the market, even if it meant hyping up a fictional relationship.

"Yeah, I do, and he has me climbing the walls every night."

"Every night, huh?"

"Yeah, every night. I'm sure you know nothing about that."

"Oh yeah? So, I just walk around with size thirteen shoes on for nothin', huh?"

I swallowed hard while rolling my peepers once more. "I think I'm pretty much done with this conversation."

Before he could respond, Suki walked up to us with

31

her eyes dead set on mine. "Hey, uh we're about to sing *Happy Birthday* and do presents, you comin'?"

"Right behind you," I told her.

"Everything good with you?" Suki asked as we walked outside.

"Me? Y—yeah, girl. I'm good."

"What was that all about back there? Seemed kind of intense."

I frowned. "That was nothing, trust me. He's a clown."

"Tell the truth, River. Did you say anything to him about me?"

"I am, and no I didn't. Trust me, the conversation or lack thereof was pointless," I assured her.

I knew nothing good was ever going to come from a man like that. Everyone around him put him on a pedestal like some sort of god or street legend, but he was simply a dog ass nigga to me.

Maverick Muhammad Malone

She brushed past me in a huff and my lips curled in amusement. I'd ruffled her pristine feathers. It was no secret River's ass didn't like me. She made that loud and clear anytime one crossed the other's path before I did my bid. I'd spent the last five years behind bars, leaving my brother to take my place at the top of East Atlanta's drug food chain. I kept my release a surprise up until twenty-four hours before. The streets didn't need to know I was back until I wanted them to. I knew the moment I showed my face at the birthday party, all of Atlanta would know of my return. As much as I knew Luca and I needed to have a one-on-one about my anticipated return to the streets, all I wanted to do was meet my niece for the first time.

"She's beautiful, man," I told Luca while watching Noemi dig into her birthday cake.

"Yeah, that's my heart right there."

"As she should be."

He nodded. "Now that you back, when we gon' talk?"

Luca turned to face me, giving me a look as if to say, *Nigga, what's good?*

33

I shot him a simple head nod. "I got you."

"When? You and I both know the streets are gonna wanna know somethin'. You a fuckin' hood celebrity out here. Everybody's gonna wanna know when you plan to take shit over, including me."

"You don't want the throne no more?" I asked him.

He shook his head. "You know I can handle it, but I also respect you and everything you put into this game and all that you taught me. It was always your seat, I was just keeping it warm for you, blood."

"I'm retiring from all that shit," I announced to him.

He snapped his neck toward me with his eyes wide. "What?"

He and I both knew he'd heard me loud and clear. I'd made the decision to keep my distance from the streets. I loved money, but if having money taught me anything, it was that no matter how much of it I had, it couldn't buy my freedom. Instead of taking my rightful seat back on the throne, I was going to put my blood, sweat, and tears into my childhood passion. Art was my first love long before I'd ever discovered the power of having money. I'd always been a good at drawing and even had a few of my own masterpieces inked onto my body. So while I was incarcerated, I started to draw everyday—didn't matter what. When I was six months away from my release date, I

34

applied for a business license with the intent to purchase a building and open my own tattoo shop when I got out. Tattooing had always been my exit plan, and now that my time had been served, I was going to execute accordingly.

"So you mean to tell me that *Triple M, M3,* the *King of East Atlanta* is really done?"

"That's factual," I nodded, "freedom tastes too good, nigga."

"When you gon' let it be known?"

"Let 'em wonder for a while. We'll make the announcement when the time is right," I told him.

"What are you gon' do now, be a personal trainer or some shit? Your ass came out swole as a mothafucka. Make a nigga wanna get back in the gym." He chuckled.

The two of us shared a laugh before turning our attention back to the party and Noemi opening her gifts. I knew I needed to get on the road soon. As happy as I was to see my brother and meet Noemi, I enjoyed my alone time and privacy.

I WALKED INTO the kitchen with my key fob in hand and aggression in my step. "Yo, Luca, I'm tryna leave and there's some old ass car in my way. I hate a mothafucka that can't park."

"What kind of car is it? I'll ask around," he told me.

"I don't know, some beat up old shit. I think it's a Hyundai or something."

"White?" River perked up.

"Yeah."

"That's mine," she said.

I chuckled. "Oh, that's your shit. Yeah, you definitely gotta get that shit out my way."

She sucked her teeth. "I was getting ready to leave anyway."

"Let's go then," I said, heading for the door.

"Hold up, didn't you get here after me? How is my car even in your way?" she asked, hot on my trail. When I didn't make an effort to respond, she continued. "Oh, so you're the one who can't park, not me."

"Whatever, I didn't plan on staying long, so I just pulled up. I don't want your raggedy ass paint on the side of my shit, so I need you to move that hunk of junk."

She frowned as we approached her car. It didn't hold

a candle to my candy apple red Range Rover, yet she chose to defend it anyway. "This is a perfectly reliable and eco-friendly car, so I don't know what you're making a big deal about it for. It gets me from point A to point B just fine."

"Yeah, aight," I brushed her off, "you and ya man have fun ridin' around the city in that."

"Fuck you, Maverick!" she yelled before slamming her door and pulling off.

I waved away the fumes from her exhaust and headed to my ride. They say that opposites attract, but the two of us repelled like opposite sides of a magnet.

"Yo, what was that about!" Luca yelled out to me before I could drive off.

I leaned my head out of my cracked window. "Shit, that? I'm just fuckin' around with her."

"River ain't the one, nigga."

"What you mean?"

"You know what I mean. She a good girl—a teacher and shit. She not fuckin' with a nigga like you."

"A teacher?" I asked, disregarding his last comment. "What she teach?"

He shrugged. "Some lil' bad mothafuckas, that's all I

know."

"I could have her if I wanted her."

Luca scoffed. "Yeah, aight."

"I'm just sayin', I ain't gon' fuck with her though. You the relationship type of nigga, not me."

"Shit, you a free man now, I don't blame you for wanting to dip your shit in the sea of pussy lining up at your doorstep, bruh," he agreed.

"You already know. *I don't love 'em, I don't chase 'em, I duck 'em*," I said, quoting Wiz Khalifa.

Luca laughed. "Aight, nigga. You gon' meet your match one day, and she gon' have you eatin' out the palm of her hand."

"That day ain't today. Be easy, I'll talk to you later," I told him before pulling off.

THREE

Two weeks later.

River

A couple weeks passed, and I still hadn't heard from Leander. The only time my phone rang was if there was a bill collector or telemarketer on the line. My heart was still broken, but the more time we went without speaking, the more I started trying to heal myself. Weaning myself from eating ice cream at any time of the day for comfort and counting down to the last day of school had become the only two things I'd pour my energy into. I pulled out my laptop, ready to spend my Friday night buried in my work, when my phone rang.

"Hello?" I answered Suki's Facetime call.

"Um, I'm trying to get in touch with my best friend. I haven't heard from her in thirty years. Her name is River Newman. Do you know her?" she asked, giving me the side eye.

I sucked my teeth. "Ha-ha. That's the exact opposite of funny, Su."

"Well damn, I've been calling you. You've been ignoring my shit like I'm some bad one-night stand."

"I haven't been ignoring you," I lied, "I've just…been caught up with work and there's a lot of stuff going on."

"Like what?"

"Ugh," I huffed. "I was going to tell you, I was just trying to process it all myself first."

"Oh my God, River, are you pregnant?" she squealed.

I frowned. "Absolutely not. In fact, I'm…single."

"Well thanks for making things awkward, sheesh. What happened to make you kick him to the curb?"

"Well…"

"Wait, you did kick *him* to the curb, right?" she

quizzed.

"Not exactly."

"Oh my God, River, you let a nigga quit you first? Have you not learned anything from me? You know you can't like a nigga until he love you. Shit ain't for play out here, okay?"

I rolled my eyes. "That's easy for you to say, you've always had someone."

"And you would too if you weren't so...y'know..."

I eyed her closely. "No, I *don't* know. Say it."

"Look, I'm not tryna come at you, aight? You my girl and I love you, and because I love you, I would be a fucked-up individual if I didn't tell you that you're pretty, River. You're fuckin' gorgeous, you're just...you're just plain as fuck." She shrugged.

My eyebrows knitted. "Excuse me?"

"Girl, do I have to break it down Barney style for you? Because I will, just say the word."

As much as I didn't feel like hearing Suki drag me, I wanted to hear what was on her mind. "Go 'head."

41

She huffed. "Fine, let's start with your hair. Your gorgeous, fuckin' long ass hair. Do you understand that bitches pay hundreds and even thousands of dollars to get hair like yours sewn into their naps? And yet, you walk around here with a bun or a ponytail when you could be givin' niggas whiplash by just letting your hair down."

I had my mother's Native Hawaiian genes to thank for my hair. As grateful as I was for my naturally long tresses, I didn't have the time or the patience to deal with it most days, so I went to my go-to styles. "Okay, fine I'll give you that. What else?"

"Well, there's also the matter of your… clothes," she said, stretching her lips wide.

"Okay, no! What about my clothes? I've stepped up my wardrobe a lot in the past couple of years!"

"Yeah, but you're still lightyears behind the rest of us. I'm not sayin' you have to be drippin' in Gucci and gold, but damn, can you try at least something with a name brand?"

"Newsflash, Su! I'm a fuckin' broke ass teacher. I don't have the luxury of having a damn kingpin for a husband to keep me dressed in designer all day, every day."

"Aht-aht! Chill with all that. Yeah, I got it good, but

I make my own money now, remember?"

I sucked my teeth. "My bad, I forgot. What is it that you do now, Su?" I asked, knowing damn well her only two talents were being bad and bougie. The girl's middle name was *Diamond* for Pete's sake. Living the luxury life was all she ever wanted.

"You know what, you're a hater, River Lynn Newman. You really don't believe me?"

"A hater? I don't have a hater bone in my body, and it's not that I don't believe you, but have you forgotten that I've known you all of my life, and I've only ever known you to have two jobs that you lasted at for all of two weeks?"

"Okay, but this is different."

"How?"

"It just is, okay? And how did we go from talking about you to talking about me, huh? Stop deflecting, River! I'm tryna show you how to get a man, a paid one at that."

I sighed. I definitely needed to win the lottery in more ways than one. "That would be nice."

"Hell yeah! You know I always got your back, girl.

So it's settled, we goin' out to catch you a baller!"

I grimaced. "When? Tonight?"

"No, it's date night tonight. Noemi can keep you company though if you want."

I looked around my apartment. There were dishes in the sink and week-old laundry that still needed to be folded. I was in no frame of mind to have company. I sighed. "As much as I love spending time with her, I think I'ma pass. I've got some more work to finish, and I'm already two glasses deep in Pinot Grigio."

"Suit yourself, girl. I'll talk to you tomorrow. Get hype, we're gon' get you a man, boo!" she said, grinning from ear to ear.

Suki had always been a kept woman. Her mother had groomed her up to be that way since she was six years old. So if anyone could hook and reel in a man, it was her.

I chuckled. "Bye, girl."

Once I hung up, I poured myself a fresh glass of wine and flopped down on the couch. If Suki insisted on finding me a man, I needed to finally begin to let go of the one I'd already lost. He'd made it clear he had no intentions of coming back, nor giving me the explanation we both knew I deserved. With my phone in hand, I went to my contacts and deleted Leander's number along with the hundreds of photos in an album saved in my camera roll. *Cheers to new beginnings,* I thought to myself.

MY PHONE VIBRATED against the coffee table, jarring me from my sleep. I looked at the screen and didn't recognize the number, so I ignored it. It was after two o'clock in the morning, and I'd fallen asleep with my laptop in my lap. I got up to stretch and carry myself from the couch to my bed when my phone began vibrating for a second time. I looked down to see the same number calling me, so I picked up.

"Hello? Who is this?"

"Don't hang up, River. It's Mav."

My forehead creased. "How did you get my number, and why the hell are you calling me so late?"

"I need you to listen to what I'm about to tell you, aight? There was an accident."

"An accident? What are you talking about?" I asked, freezing in my step.

"Luca and Suki."

45

"Oh, my God! Are they okay?"

"I don't know much. I'm on my way to Emory University Hospital right now."

"Okay, okay! I'm on my way!"

I RUSHED IN through the emergency room doors and saw Maverick standing there. Before I could part my lips to ask for an update, he spoke up, "It's too late."

I swallowed hard at a tangle of words lodged in my throat. "W—what?"

His words stole the wind right out of my chest. I reached out for the closest chair to me, grabbing the arms for stability. My throat squeezed down on a scream as pain overflowed from my heart. Hearing the news that my best friend was dead made my world spin on every axis. My heart palpitations, numbness of my fingertips, and the spinning room were sure signs that I could pass out any moment.

"How—how bad was it?" I asked him.

He shook his head. "You don't want to know all that."

"Please," I begged, choking back tears.

46

Maverick drew in a deep breath. His eyes hung low as he made his way over to sit beside me. "Both their bodies were a maze of cuts and bruises. There were severe puncture wounds and disfigurement due to the high speed the other car was going at the time of impact. They were both pronounced dead at the scene."

"No. No. No! No! No!"

"Suki's body was found ejected from the vehicle. She wasn't wearing a seatbelt."

There was a sudden tightness in my chest, followed by a hollow feeling in my stomach as if I was on a nonstop rollercoaster. Everything felt surreal.

"St—stop. Stop talking," I said, grabbing my chest.

"You said you wanted to know," he reminded me.

My foot bounced against the floor in a neck-and-neck competition with my fleeting heartbeat. "I—I"

"Are you okay?"

Those three words were the last I heard before everything went black.

I WOKE UP in a hospital bed with an IV in my arm pumping fluids into me without my knowledge. I slowly lifted my arm before turning to see Mav standing in the corner. It was then that I'd realized what had happened. Everything came flooding back.

"Tell me it's all a dream," I begged him.

"More like a nightmare," he replied.

Yet again, my world had stopped spinning. I shifted in the bed, unable to get comfortable in more ways than one. The massive headache was occupying every inch of my head, disabling me from asking all of the questions I wanted to.

"What happened?" I asked, massaging my temples.

"You passed out in the waiting room. Doctor said you were dehydrated."

"Oh," I said, shaking my head. I had all those glasses of wine to thank for that. "Where's Noemi?" I asked him. "Does she know?"

He shook his head. "She's at home in her bed with the babysitter there, unharmed, with no knowledge of what happened to her parents."

I took a brief sigh of relief before the reality sunk in about how sad it would be when she did find out the truth. She loved her parents just as much as they loved her.

"There's more to the story I think you should know," he told me, prying me away from my private thoughts.

I eyed him hesitantly, unsure if I could take anymore. "What is it?"

"They told me that narcotic residue and liquor were present in the vehicle."

My forehead creased. "What? Suki didn't do drugs. She, I mean, what the hell?"

"Luca did a lot of things in his life, but he's my brother, and I know he'd never drive hot like that. Something isn't right about any of this."

"What do you mean?"

"I mean, I don't think this was an accident."

My eyes widened. "Are you saying what I think you're saying?"

"I think they were murdered," he told me.

49

Suddenly my mouth went dry. Before I could even formulate a response, the nurse came in with another lady behind her.

"How are you feeling, ma'am?" the nurse asked.

I nodded. "I've got a headache, but I'm okay."

"Good, well I'll get you some Tylenol and have the doctor come in to check you out before I draw up your discharge papers."

"Thank you."

"This is Miss Kathy Jenner. She's a social worker. She'd like to speak with the two of you."

I shot a glance over at Maverick, who shifted his weight from one foot to the other. "About what?" he asked.

"Which of you is a blood relative to either of the deceased?" the social worker asked.

"I am," he said.

"And I understand that they had a child."

"What is this about?" I interjected.

She kept her attention on Maverick. "Being that you are the closest blood relative, and we could not get in touch with anyone else, we are temporarily awarding you custodial rights to the child."

"What? I may not be blood, but I'm her godmother."

"And I'm her uncle," he said, cutting me off. "My brother would want her to be with me."

I frowned. "What do you know about raising a child? You've been in her life for all of two seconds. She doesn't even know you!"

Before Maverick could respond, Miss Jenner spoke up again. "Please remember that this is temporary. There is a court date set in a week where a judge will iron out more details of custody over the minor."

"So, that's it? She just goes to live with him until the court date?"

"Yes, but I must caution you both. There is a lot of trauma associated with losing both parents at the same time, no matter how old the child is."

"She's five," I told her.

Miss Jenner nodded. "At such a young age, she

51

won't fully be able to process her feelings and may begin to act out in other ways."

"Like what?" I asked.

"Well, in my years of doing this, I've seen cases of regression, night terrors, trouble eating or sleeping, not talking or doing things she'd normally do. I even suggest a therapist to help her talk out her feelings."

"She don't need a fuckin' therapist. She gon' be with family. She'll be good," Maverick told her.

I huffed, too weak and mentally spent to argue anymore. He was ignorant as fuck, and I wanted to scream to the top of my lungs. He didn't know shit about Noemi, yet he thought simply being her blood relative made him overly qualified for the job. I wanted nothing more than to sit back and watch his overly confident ass fall flat on his face, but him failing meant Noemi could suffer, and I couldn't sit back and let that happen.

TIME FELT LIKE it was dragging as I sat in the middle of my bedroom floor surrounded by used tissues filled with tears and a box of old memories of Suki and I over the years. I hadn't eaten anything since leaving the hospital twelve hours prior. I still felt so weak inside; unable to do anything but sleep and cry.

52

The familiar sound of the factory iPhone ringtone cut through the silence. I wiped my puffy eyes before reaching over to see who was calling. As soon as I pressed accept for Maverick, I could hear Noemi crying in the background.

"Hello?"

"I don't know what she likes to eat. She's crying. She's asking questions I don't have the answers to."

"That's because she doesn't know you," I reminded him.

"I didn't call to hear you talk shit."

"Then what did you call for because sarcasm, anger, and grief are all I have right now."

"I called because I need your help, but fuck it, I'll figure shit out on my own," he said before hanging up.

I didn't know whether to be insulted that he'd hung up in my face or delighted in the fact that he'd gotten what he deserved by thinking being with Noemi would be a piece of cake. She was giving him a run for his money. Instead of letting him get to me, I decided to throw his ass a bone and shoot him a quick text.

Me: [6:13pm]: Her favorite food is Mac and Cheese.

Instead of having the common courtesy to thank me, he opted to just "like" my message instead. "Fuckin' jerk," I mumbled to myself.

Ten minutes later, I got another text from him. *"River, a nigga ain't one to beg, but I need your help. She won't eat. She won't go to bed. She won't do shit but cry."*

I sighed. As much as I wanted to leave his ass on read, I had to be the bigger person out of the two of us. We were all hurting, but Noemi had to be our number one priority. *"Getting in the shower now, then on my way,"* I responded.

THE MOMENT I pulled into Luca and Suki's driveway, a chilling feeling washed over me. It was the first time I'd have to prepare myself to go step into their home and not see either one of them in the flesh. My heart dropped the moment Maverick swung open the front door, and I saw Noemi sitting on the bottom step crying her eyes out.

"Why all the tears, baby girl?" I asked.

Instead of responding, she ran over to me and

buried her head into the crevice between my shoulder and neck, wetting it with fresh tears. I hugged her as tight as my weak arms could, secretly promising myself that I'd never let her go.

"Where are Mommy and Daddy?" she asked. "When are they coming back?"

I glanced over her shoulder at Maverick whose gaze was ping-ponging, avoiding direct eye contact with either of us. He hadn't told her a thing and from the looks of it, he didn't plan to.

"The most important thing to know is that both your Mommy and Daddy love you very much. Did you eat anything?"

"No."

"Come on and let's get you fed, and then I'll give you a bath, tuck you in as snug as a bug in a rug, and read you a story. How's that sound?" I asked her.

A ghost of a smile crept across her face as she nodded. At least the waterworks had stopped. "Go in the kitchen, and I'll meet you in there in a minute, okay?"

Once she was out of earshot, I turned my attention to Maverick. Although his lips were shut, his body language was coming in loud and clear. From his awkward stance to the tight look on his face, it was easy to see he was out of his element.

"You still haven't told her?" I whispered.

He shook his head. "What the fuck am I supposed to tell her?"

"The truth. She's five. She's going to want to know her parents aren't coming back. She deserves that from you."

"I can't tell her that. Tonight has been hell. She already hates me."

I sighed. "She doesn't hate you. Her world is literally about to be turned upside down when she finds out what happened. Just give her time to learn her new normal and get to know you as her uncle and not the man whose suddenly just in her home without her parents."

"I can't be the one to break her heart," he admitted.

"If the roles were reversed and Noemi was your child, what would you want Luca to do?" I quizzed.

He stood silent with his forehead crinkled like a paper fan. He was either thinking or he already knew the answer. "You cook, I'll talk. Deal?"

Surprised, I tilted my head to the side before nodding. "Deal...I guess."

He followed me into the kitchen, where I had a good sightline of Noemi sitting in the living room on her iPad. "So, you said her favorite food is mac and cheese?"

I nodded before washing my hands and making my way around the kitchen to pull out everything I needed. Once the water began to boil, I poured in the macaroni noodles shaped like different characters from Frozen. Eight minutes later, I was completely done.

"See? It's simple, just read the box. It's Kraft Mac and Cheese, Mav, not rocket science.

Here, taste it," I said, handing him a spoon. There was no way I was about to hold it up to his lips and feed him like a king.

He eyed me closely before scooping some out onto the spoon and shoveling it into his mouth. "Damn, for two dollars a box, this shit hit."

"Noemi, come and eat. There's something Uncle Maverick and I want to talk to you about."

"Mav," he corrected me, "just Mav."

Once Noemi was seated, we sat on opposite sides of her and watched her eat in silence for a few seconds. I was sure neither of us knew the first thing about talking to a young child about death and the many faces of grief. We were both in unchartered waters. As much as we wanted to soften the blow, we had to tell her the truth.

"You uh, you remember when you asked where your mommy and daddy were?" I began.

"Yeah."

"And you remember when you asked when they were coming home?"

She chewed. "Mmhm."

"Well, um, they—"

"They aren't coming back," Mav interjected.

Her brow furrowed. "Why not? Why didn't I go?"

"Baby girl, when people…when people die, they don't uh, they don't come back home," I told her, choking back my own set of tears.

"You mean never?"

I shook my head. "Never. Your mommy and daddy died, and when that happens, their uh, their heart stops beating and they—we uh, we won't be able to see them anymore with our eyes."

"But where did they go?"

"You remember last year when your goldfish, Dr. Bubbles, died and you, me, your mommy and your daddy had a funeral for him and then he went to be with his other fish friends in the sky?"

Noemi nodded. "They're with Dr. Bubbles?" she asked, her voice wavering with confusion and distress.

I let out a sharp sigh. "Yes, they're in the sky with Dr. Bubbles. But guess what?" I asked, wiping my tears. "There are so many people that are here with you that love you, okay? Your Mimi and Papa love you. I love you. Your Uncle Mav loves you. You will always be taken care of."

"As long as I'm breathing, you'll never want for anything," Mav promised her.

"I want to watch TV," Noemi said, pushing away from the table.

"Wait—"

"No, it's fine, let her go," I told him, "she needs to process this however she's going to process this."

We were all processing their deaths in tiny bits and pieces and in different ways. There was no way I expected a five-year old to process the intricacies of death after one

59

conversation. After cleaning the kitchen, giving Noemi a bath, and tucking her in, I was spent. I leaned down to kiss her forehead.

"Goodnight and sweet dreams, baby girl."

"No!" she yelled, grabbing onto my arm. "Don't leave, he's mean."

"He's not mean, he's just…he just misses your daddy very much, but I promise he loves you a whole lot, okay?"

"Please don't go!" she cried.

I sighed. "You've gotta go to bed and so do I. I have school in the morning just like you do."

"Please?"

"Do you want me to spend the night? Would that make you feel better?" I asked, watching her slow smile build as the seconds fleeted past us.

"Yes!"

"Okay, well let me go talk to your Uncle Mav about it, okay? I'll be right back," I said before leaving her bedroom. I couldn't leave her hanging. My heart wouldn't let me. I walked down the hallway and saw Mav coming up the stairs.

"Is she asleep?" he asked.

"Not yet. She wants me to spend the night, but I told her I would talk to you about it first. I'm not trying to crowd your space."

"Uh yeah, you can take the guest room across the hall from her if you want."

"Nah, the couch is fine with me. To be honest, it's fuckin' creepy being here, y'know? Without them…"

He nodded. "Yeah, I feel it too."

"I'll stay in her room until she falls asleep, then I'll make my way to the couch."

"Cool, night," he said, before turning to head back downstairs.

"Goodnight…"

Mav

It had been almost a week since the accident, and I was still gathering my peace in pieces. I'd been dipping in and out of my grief since I first got the news that my baby brother was dead. My head was stuck in a weird space— wandering in and out of a fog as I questioned what the fuck life really was. I had no problem processing death. I'd seen niggas come and go so much that it never fazed me, but losing my blood hit different. I'd been absent for the past five years of his life. He'd become a father and a husband in that time, and just when we got the chance to reconnect, he was taken from me.

I got to the church early and stood next to the first pew staring at the two bullet gold caskets in front of me. With my feet planted at the end of Luca's closed casket, I reached out and put my hand on it. Gone too soon was an understatement. Nothing about his death sat well with me. I was angry at myself for not taking the streets back under my control, thinking that may have saved him. My emerging thoughts did nothing to stop the fertile ground for thoughts of revenge. I drew in a frustrated breath as tears streaked down my face. I didn't know who was living inside my body because everything felt foreign. Nothing felt recognizable. Nothing felt like home. I glanced over at Suki's closed casket and shook my head. If only he'd *never married her.* Suki was the type of bitch I could never trust. She was the type to know gold when it glittered. I told Luca about her from the moment he brought her around me. I knew she was a no-good female, but he was the type to wear his heart on his sleeve, consequences be damned.

I quickly swiped my hand over my face, wiping away the tears when I heard someone walk up behind me.

"People are starting to come in," River told me, "do you need more time? I can try to hold them off for a little while longer."

I shook my head. "Nah, let 'em in."

River

I felt lethargic throughout the entire sermon, itching to get out of that church and away from any and every one I could. There was only so much sympathy I could take. As soon as the funeral ended, I walked over to give Suki's mother a hug. She took the news so hard, she was almost no help to me when helping to plan the funeral.

"Mrs. Lawrence, hi," I said, walking up to her.

She reached out and grabbed my hands. "River, thank you so much for everything. I know I've been hard to work with."

"It's understandable. You don't ever have to apologize to me for that. It's my job to help with anything I can. Suki is...we were best friends."

"Can I talk to you about something important, River?" she asked, leaning in to speak lower.

"Yes, ma'am."

"How are you feeling about Noemi being with...him," she whispered, nodding her head in Maverick's direction.

"Uh, I mean, maybe I had my reservations at first, but they're warming up to each other."

"Well, I have my own reservations."

"Like what?"

She frowned, folding her freshly manicured nails across her crisp, black dress. "I just don't feel like Noemi is safe with him. I mean, look at him. All those tattoos—I don't want Noemi growing up under a man like that."

"With all due respect, Mrs. Lawrence, Noemi's father had tattoos too. Maybe not as many, but it's nothing foreign to her."

She huffed. "So, you trust him over us? Her own blood?"

I could tell that she was trying to take the conversation in a direction I didn't want to go in, so I decided to put a stop to it before she went any further. "He's her blood too," I reminded her, "and right now, he's the closest thing to a home that she's got since you and Mr. Lawrence live three hours away, so…"

"Well, I'm going to see what can be done about this, you just wait and see!"

She took a sharp turn and walked off. I was already over the entire day and conversation, so her storming off didn't faze me one bit. Prior to our conversation, Maverick had agreed that Suki's parents could take her for a few days while the two of us scheduled some time to clean out their house and move all of Noemi's things into his house. I didn't know whether or not to warn him about Suki's mother's threat or just chalk it up to her grieving. Nevertheless, I needed some fresh air.

I saw Maverick standing off to the side and could see the tattoo across his collarbone peeking through the unbuttoned part of his button up shirt. I made my way over to him. "Get me out of here?" I asked as more of a command than a question.

"Let's go."

Without uttering another syllable, I followed him out to his car and slid my back against the burnt orange leather seat. Just before he pulled off, a man approached his car and waved for him to roll down his window.

"Who are you?" Mav asked, eyeing him closely.

"Hi, I've been trying to reach out to you—to both of you. I'm Dominic Gregory, the deceased couple's lawyer. They had an estate plan. Please come to my office tomorrow morning at ten o'clock, and I'll explain everything," he said, extending two of his business cards to Mav.

He looked at it and then passed one to me. "Bet," Mav said before revving his engine and speeding out of the parking lot.

Neither of us uttered a sound until we got on the interstate. He let the windows down and I let the wind dry my tears. I turned to look at him as he turned the stereo up, letting Tupac's melodic voice rap the lyrics to *I Ain't Mad At Cha.* Simultaneously, we began to bob our heads. Mav reached into his console and pulled out a blunt and a lighter.

"Light it for me," he mumbled, extending his hand to me.

My forehead creased. "I don't smoke."

"You ain't gotta hit it but once, just light it. You know how, right?"

I rolled my eyes. "Yes, I know how to light a damn blunt."

"Do it then."

I took the tightly rolled blunt and lifted it to my lips while Mav rolled the windows up and opened the sunroof. The lighter sparked and I inhaled, igniting the tip of the blunt. I instantly felt lightheaded and started coughing my head off while passing the blunt back his way.

"You good?" he asked, chuckling in between each word.

"What the fuck is that? That's strong as fuck!" I said, smacking my chest as he sped down 285.

"Blue Dream," he said before he inhaled the potent drug.

As pretty as it sounded, I was no match for it. I'd always been a poor smoker. Truthfully, anything outside the realm of wine was all too rich for my blood. Once I caught my breath and the burning in my chest started to subside, I turned my attention to him.

"What are we going to do?"

Taking his eyes off the road, he glanced at me. "Whatever we gotta do," he said before turning the music down.

"I mean, I've got a lot on my plate right now. I—I don't know if I can do this. I'm grieving, I've got a broken h—never mind. I—this is all just a fuckin' lot for me and yet you're sitting over there as cool as a cucumber. Do you not feel anything?"

"I'm grieving too. I just don't sit around and cry like you do."

"Mmm. My mama always said you can tell the heart of a man by how he grieves."

"Your mama don't know shit about me," he retorted.

I frowned. "Well excuse me for mourning my best friend like a normal fuckin' person. If anyone was to understand that I thought it would've been you, but I guess not. What the hell is wrong with you? It's like you're from a different fuckin' planet or somethin'! All I want to do is get to a point where the pain stops. I just need it all to fuckin' stop!"

"It never stops, River. You just learn to ignore it or make room for it."

Surprised at the darkness of his comment, I drew in a sharp breath. "That's dark as fuck...you do know that, right?"

He lazily shrugged his shoulder. "It's the truth."

I sunk into the seat, no longer wanting to converse for the rest of the ride. "It's just right up here on the left," I spoke up as he neared my apartment building.

He pulled up and put the car in park. "Thanks for the ride."

"Yup." He nodded, before ashing his blunt out of the window.

"Okay, well goodnight," I said, exiting the car.

"Yeah," he said before driving off.

I huffed. He didn't even have the basic know how to make sure I got inside my apartment safely. The more time I spent around him, the more he proved me right. He was *still* a dog ass nigga.

River

I sat in the waiting room flipping through a Better Homes and Gardens magazine from 2017. It was almost time for our appointment with the lawyer, and Maverick was nowhere to be found. Annoyed, I pulled out my phone to text him.

Me: [9:55am]: *Our meeting with the lawyer is in five minutes. What's your ETA?*

Mav: [9:56am]:*I'll be there.*

He was just as nonchalant through text as he was in the flesh. I'd never met someone who got underneath my skin so easily. If I was Superman, Maverick would be my kryptonite.

"Miss Newman?" a man's voice asked behind me.

I turned to see the lawyer standing there. "Good morning, Mr. Gregory."

"Good morning and thank you for joining me on such short notice. Is Mr. Malone going to be joining us as well?"

"Um, yeah he's just running a little behind, but he'll be here."

"I'm right here," Maverick's voice boomed behind me.

Goosebumps coated my exposed arms as I screamed on the inside. There he was, swooping in a hero, when I seemed to be the only one who knew he was really the villain.

"Good morning, Mr. Malone, let's go ahead and get started. I'll read the will and testament the deceased couple filed in the event of their passing. You both were named, so that is why both of you are here today."

He cleared his throat before beginning, "Being of sound mind and body do hereby make this to be our last will and testament. We hereby appoint Maverick Muhammad Malone as the legal guardian of our daughter, Noemi Milan Malone. We also hereby name River Newman as co-guardian and as the guardian of Noemi's estate. We divide all of the remainder of our gross estate to Noemi Milan Malone. All of our assets will be held in an estate in her name and overseen by River Newman."

"Um, I'm sorry to interrupt, but what does that mean exactly?" I interjected.

"It means that Noemi will have access to the multiple accounts when she turns eighteen years old, but until then, you are the guardian of everything regarding her financial well-being. I'll gather an inclusive lists of all of the accounts and email them to you before close of business today."

"Okay, and it also said something about co-guardian. What does that mean exactly?"

"Although Mr. Malone will be her legal guardian appointed by the court, you also will have rights to the child and assist in her upbringing in whatever format that you two discuss. In any matter, being that both of you were named in regards to taking care of a minor, you will have to work together."

I nodded. "I see."

All I had to do was play nice for the remainder of the meeting. I sat back, awaiting the time where I could scream to the heavens alone in my car. Work together? Did he know who the fuck he was talking to? We could barely be in the same space together for fifteen minutes before one of us set the other off. How the hell were we going to work together to raise a five-year-old?

"Can we get copies of all of this for our records?" I asked.

He cleared his throat. "Certainly, but that's not all I have to share."

"What else is there?" Maverick spoke up for the first time.

"I got a call about fifteen minutes before you walked in today. There's a third party with legitimate interests that has stepped forward and petitioned the court for custody over the child."

"What?" he roared.

"Who?" I quizzed.

"Um, a Mrs. Brinelda Lawrence."

"Suki's mother," I mumbled while shaking my head. It seemed that her threat wasn't an empty promise or grief at all.

Maverick's fists tightened. "What?"

"As a rule, the court typically honors the parent's wishes and appoints their nominee, but in rare cases there have been times where the judge can choose someone else if the fitness of the nominee is questioned. And given your record, I would be lying if I told you that they didn't have a case," he informed us.

"Is there anything he can do?"

"Well, the good news is, it's highly unlikely that she would end up a ward of the state or entered into the system. I also think that the two of you together will show the court that there is still stability in the household with two guardians."

"But we don't live together," I corrected him.

"Shit, we barely like each other," Maverick griped.

I rolled my eyes. "Is that going to pose a problem?"

He shifted his tie. "Listen, I'm not going to tell you two how to figure things out because that's completely at your discretion, but I will say, the more stability you can show, the better at least leading up to the court date. Once that's over, you two can make whatever arrangements suit you best."

"When is the court date?"

"It's on the docket for December."

"That's six months from now!" I exclaimed.

"Again, I can't tell you what to do. You two will have to make your own decisions, but just remember to do what is best for the child."

MAVERICK AND I stood face-to-face in the parking lot with matching manila folders in our hands. "I mean, wow, they've already got so much money put away for her college," I said, flipping through some of the documents, "but what if she doesn't want to go to college?"

"She'll go simply because liberal arts will grow her mind, but it's business and science that will keep food on her table and a roof over her head. She'll need them both to survive out here."

"It says here that she has over two-hundred shares in Amazon, Apple, and Tesla."

"Baby girl is set, and she doesn't even know it yet."

"It's almost like they were preparing to d—die…" I said, choking out the last word.

He shrugged. "Livin' his lifestyle, he'd be a fool not to. Nothing lasts forever. Ain't no such thing as immortality when you do your business in the streets."

"So, I feel like it's no secret we have a lot to discuss. When did you want to do that? I'm free after 3:30 throughout the week. Weekends, I usually don't have plans either."

"For somebody with a man, you sure sound like you got a lot of free time on your hand."

I tried to let his snide comment roll right off me and make sure we stayed on topic. "Like I was saying, the sooner we hash this shit out the better, so maybe I'll come back over this evening."

"Bet. You cookin'?"

The *fuckin' nerve* of this nigga. "What?" I asked, snapping my neck to the side.

"A nigga gon' be hungry."

I rolled my eyes. "You and I both know you have the means to have anything you want for dinner."

"Money can't buy everything."

"Bye, Mav."

"Later."

Mav

I hopped back in my car and tossed the folder onto my passenger seat before starting the engine. Since there would be a child occupying my space on a daily basis, I had to make sure I removed the gun to the safe instead of keeping it next to me at all times during the day and in my nightstand at night. Before prison, I was so used to getting everything I wanted, coming out I didn't expect things to be different. Yet, it seemed overnight I'd gone from the hood to fatherhood, and Noemi hadn't made it easy for me. Playing mommy and daddy wasn't my style, but the truth was I needed River. I couldn't act like she didn't save my ass. I knew the stains on my record would come back to haunt me one day, but I didn't think they'd get in the way of me being able to honor my brother's dying request. I had to make sure she was brought up right. I owed her that. River and I both did. She was a child left without her parents; and there was nothing sadder than that.

LATER THAT EVENING, River walked into the foyer and frowned at all the stacked cardboard boxes filling the space. "Um, what are you doing?"

"Packing up Noemi's stuff. I can't stay in this house another night. And now that we know she's going to be with me full-time, I think it's time to move things to my place," I told her, carrying another box down the stairs.

I'd been packing up for hours, determined not to spend another night in the house where my brother used to rest his head.

She sighed. "I thought we were going to talk."

"You can't talk and pack a box at the same time?" I asked. She dramatically rolled her eyes, and I smirked. It was too easy to get under River's skin. So easy that it was fun to me. The shit was easily becoming one of my favorite pastimes.

"I'm just saying, does it have to be tonight?"

"What better time than tonight?"

"I don't know, maybe tomorrow or the next day?

79

I'm tired, and I have too much going on right now to just drop everything and be—"

"According to the paperwork, they gave instructions to put the house on the market within sixty days of their passing," I said, hitting her with straight facts.

She stared at me, slowly trying to swallow the backlog of words in her throat. I knew she hadn't expected for me to read through the documents. She really didn't know the type of nigga I was or who she was fuckin' with. "Fine."

It felt weird rummaging through their things and having a say on what got to go where, but it had to be done. River cracked open a cardboard box in the living room and began wrapping and packing up their family photos. "Wow, I remember this night clearly. It was the night they got engaged. I even took the picture," River said, picking up another framed photo. "Oh wow, look at this. This was from their wedding day. She was so round and didn't even care. They were both so happy that day," she said, getting teary-eyed.

I had already been locked up by then, so there wasn't much I could say. I couldn't relate. "Wish I could've been there."

"Why? If I recall correctly you called your brother a

fool the night he proposed."

"And I still feel that way. Some things don't change."

"Yeah, especially not you."

"Yo, before we go any further, you gotta put your beef out on the table. You walk around with this big ass stick up your ass whenever I'm around, itching to judge a nigga that you know nothing about."

She huffed. "Trust me, I know everything I *need* to know about you."

"That's where you're wrong."

"All I'm saying is I don't see how you can change my mind about the type of person who would sneak around with his own flesh and blood's woman."

"And what about a woman who would *sneak around* with her man's flesh and blood? You were thick as fuckin' thieves with one of them though, right? So, what does that say about you?"

"That's not the point, and you know it. Besides, she heard it from me, too. I told her she was wrong for being a part of whatever the fuck you two had going on behind Luca's back."

"So, that's what all the negativity you've been

throwin' my way is all about? You really think I had something goin' on with my brother's girl?"

"Look, you can deny it all you want to try and make yourself feel better or whatever, but I was there just like you were that that night, and I heard what I heard."

"Oh, I remember that night clearly and there ain't nothin' to deny. I'll always own up to my shit."

"Yeah, okay," she said, rolling her eyes, "so you two were never fuckin' around behind Luca's back?"

"No, that's not the case at all."

"Then what was it between you two because I'm not crazy. I know what I heard, and it didn't sound like an innocent conversation."

"You want details?"

"Yeah, I do."

I sucked my teeth. She wanted me to paint the full picture for her, so that's what she'd get. "You can stick to the narrative in your head about me, or you can quit bumpin' ya gums and listen to what the fuck really happened that night."

"Fine, I'm listening," she said, tightly folding her arms across her chest.

"I was out at a club on the Nawfside one night. It's lit with bottles everywhere. The liquor's flowing freely, so niggas is sneakin' and geekin'. Somehow, she ended up in my section. I'm chillin' in the cut, enjoyin' myself. I didn't need to be flashy. Beggars and ballers alike knew my name, you know? She made her way over to me, and by that point, I'm seein' double, and again, just tryna have a good time. I wasn't botherin' nobody. We start talkin' a bit, one thing led to another and boom, your girl topped me off in the parking lot. We went and got a room, I knocked her off and that was that. A few months later, she's on Luca's arm cheesin' in my face like we never met. When he told me she was pregnant, I started to question the timeline and approached her about it. What you heard that night was me making her get a paternity test without my brother's knowledge."

Her eyebrows drew close together. "Is Noemi your daughter, Maverick?"

Her tone rested on pins and needles as she waited for me to give her another reason to hate me. "She's not mine, River."

She sighed, and then proceeded to open her mouth once more. "But wait—she…she told me that she broke things off with you that night."

"What was there to break off, River? That's far from the fuckin' truth. All I wanted to do was make sure she wasn't carrying my seed. That's all it ever was for me from the beginning. A bitch like that could never get nothin' from me besides broken off, and that's if I'm feelin' generous."

"Okay, okay. I'm sorry, alright?"

"Keep your half ass apology, and maybe next time ask before you assume."

"I—you know what, fine. Maybe I let my imagination run rapid, but she said what she said, and I took her for her word because that's my girl. Why would she ever have to lie to me?"

"Clout. Power. When mothafuckas get even a little whiff of money, they never wanna go back to broke. So what do they do? They do whatever the fuck it take to stay in the presence of a fuckin' dollar bill."

River

Telling little white lies had always been one of Suki's quirks. Like most, she'd only do them when it benefitted her. But this…this was more than a little lie. Her lie had fanned the flames of my hatred for a man who didn't deserve my negativity. Years had gone by, and I'd never gotten the full story or the truth from Suki.

"I don't know…"

He frowned. "What is there not to know when you know the truth? Unless you don't believe me."

"I'm not sayin' that. I'm just sayin' it doesn't sound like the Suki I knew, that's all."

84

"People show you who they want you to see. Whatever benefits them in the moment is what they'll portray."

Even though we both knew he was giving a word, I wasn't going to give him the satisfaction. I lowkey feel like an idiot for not knowing the full story all these years. Knowing the truth, there was nothing else I could do except for humble myself and apologize.

"I've hated you for a long time…for nothing," I admitted.

"I know."

I frowned. "What?"

"I said I know."

"I apologize…and I actually mean it this time. I misjudged you without having the full story."

He let out a long, slow exhale. "Yeah, aight."

I shook my head, feeling my eyelids about to give way to tears. "I just—I feel bad because like I'm your best friend. Why would you feel like you needed to lie to me?"

"Yo, you mad sensitive."

I sucked my teeth. I was done using him as my sounding board. Our whole conversation had done nothing but make me feel like a terrible friend. What was wrong with me that she felt like she couldn't tell me what really went on between her and Maverick? The more I sat and thought about it, I started to understand her reasoning. It was the same reason I didn't come crying to her about my breakup with Leander. It was the embarrassment behind it all. Nobody likes to feel played, especially when you're used to being in control.

"Look, I know that's your friend, and I don't like to speak ill of the dead, but that bitch had the charm of a cockroach. How did the two of you even become friends in the first place? You're nothing alike."

"Watch your fuckin' mouth! I don't play behind my girl, aight? She wasn't this bad person that you're trying to paint her out to be. Yeah, she had flaws, but who doesn't? She may have done some fucked up shit, but she loved your brother and she loved Noemi, and that's all that matters at the end of the day!"

"Yeah, she may have loved him, but I told Luca a bitch like that would be the death of him."

"Excuse me? Why the fuck would you say something like that?" I fumed.

"All I'm sayin' is, after I found out the baby wasn't mine, I got set up and was being hauled off to prison a month later."

I scowled at him. "Where exactly are you going with this?"

"I warned him about her, and he didn't listen. Fool always did wear his heart on his sleeve."

86

"Again, there you go painting my girl out like she's some she-devil just lookin' for a quick come-up."

"That's exactly what I'm sayin', and I'm also sayin' my brother was too deep in the pussy to see it for what it really was. Had she not been fuckin' around with more than one nigga at a time, there would've been no need for her to get a paternity test in the first place. You go from my dick to another in the matter of a month, maybe even weeks. What that tell you?"

"I mean, name one person that's perfect though, and in the same breath, isn't love about sacrifice? I'm sure they both sacrificed a lot to get to the happy place that they were in. No matter all the bullshit they had to go through to be happy, they came out on top in the end."

"No, they didn't. they ended up six feet under. That's what being *in love* got them. And you know why? Because love is the pinnacle of human downfall, River. Love exposes your weaknesses to your enemies and being in it only elevates your stress levels. You stay wonderin', *Oh, does he love me? Is he fuckin' another bitch*, all that, and for what? Tell me one good thing that's ever come from two mothafuckas in love!"

"Noemi," I rebutted.

He glared at me. The silence alone brought me satisfaction. I'd made him eat his words. "At the end of the day, I'd rather be respected than loved. Love make a mothafucka act outside himself, and I'm not about that shit."

"Spoken like someone whose had his heart broken one too many times," I jabbed.

"Never."

"Hmph! And exactly how many times have you been in love?"

"None," he boasted.

"And you think that makes you a better man?" I quizzed.

"Not better, smarter," he corrected me.

I rolled my eyes as my arms shot up over my head. "Oh, my God! You're such a pseudo intellectual when it comes to any and everything about love!"

"What the fuck does that mean?"

"It means you talk a good game like you really know shit, but the truth is, if true love was standing right in front of you, you wouldn't know the first thing to do with it."

He chuckled before picking up two boxes and walking out of my sight. "The world may never know."

He walked away and left me screaming on the inside. Even after finding out the truth, he may not have been the dog ass nigga I thought he once was, but he still wasn't about shit. His ideology on love alone was enough to send me running the other way. If our conversation taught me anything, it was that we would *never* be on that level.

River

I'd picked up Noemi from Suki's parents and brought her to Maverick's house. It was my first time coming to his place, and I was pleasantly surprised when I pulled into a gated neighborhood in the high-end part of the city.

"5715...5715," I mumbled, darting my eyes from one side of the road to the other so that I wouldn't drive past his house.

I pulled into the driveway of a large white house, with a dark roof, black garage doors and front door. The landscaping was fresh, including a freshly cut yard and a colorful flower bed surrounding the mailbox. I definitely never pegged him as someone living in "suburbia," but I was happy to see there wouldn't be a downgrade in Noemi's living arrangements. I pulled up beside his Range Rover that was backed in and killed the engine.

"Let's go, Kiddo! We're here." With Noemi's bookbag flung over my shoulder, we walked up to his door and rang the doorbell.

"Where are we?" she asked, gripping my hand.

"This is your Uncle Mav's house."

"Why didn't we go to my house?" Noemi asked.

"This is where you're going to stay now, with your Uncle Mav."

"And you, too?"

I quickly shook my head. "No, I don't live here."

She pouted. "But I don't want to live here. I want to go back to my house."

Before I could respond, the large door opened. Mav stood there with a sweaty brow and even sweatier wife beater. "Come in."

"Is now a bad time?"

"Nah, I was just out in the garage working out."

"Okay," I said, scanning my surroundings.

Cherry wood floors ran from the front of the house straight to the back. Each room in my immediate view was large but didn't have much furniture in it. He was clearly a minimalist. I could already tell he was going to have to do a lot to make his house feel like a home to her. Currently, there was no warmth in it at all, even with the oversized windows toward the back of the house letting in tons of natural light.

"You wanna go put your stuff in your room?" he asked Noemi.

"That sounds like a good idea. Where is her room?" I asked, snapping back into the present.

"Up the stairs, second door on the left."

I turned to Noemi and smiled. "I'll race you. Ready, set, go!"

Noemi ran up the staircase, hand gliding up the railing as I stayed hot on her trail taking two stairs at once. She burst open the door to see that her bedroom set had been delivered and there was a half-drawn mural on the wall directly across from her bed. I could see Noemi's name spelled out in an arch over a half-sketched unicorn that took up the majority of the center.

"Wow, you had someone come in and do this?"

"I did it."

"What? No you didn't, stop lying."

"I'm not lying," he said, his face emotionless.

"Damn, I didn't know you could draw...like you just don't look like, you know what, never mind. It's dope."

"Thanks, but uh, I'm gonna get back to my workout. I'll leave y'all to it," he said before turning to leave.

"Isn't this cool, Noemi? I bet you've got the coolest room on the whole block!"

She smiled. "It's pretty."

"It is, and see, all your things are here now, and you can decorate however you want."

"I still miss my old room," she said, eyes falling to her shoes.

"I know, but you'll learn to love your new room, I promise. You'll get used to it and it'll become your new favorite place to be."

"Will you stay with me?"

I sighed. "Um, I don't know. I'd have to ask your Uncle Mav again. But enough of that for now, let's say we get some fresh air and take a spin in one of your luxurious rides? Your uncle told me they were all parked in the garage. How's that sound?"

She smiled. "I like you being here."

"Well, I love spending time with you, Kiddo. Now, go put your stuff down and let's go," I said, flipping my sunshades back over my eyes.

Noemi and I made our way out to the garage to see a stockpile of toilet paper and other household products.

"Um, is there a pending zombie attack I'm unaware of?" I asked Maverick, who was standing on the other end of the two-car garage lifting weights.

"I got five and a half bathrooms in my house. A nigga can never have too much toilet paper."

I rolled my eyes. His ass seemed to have a smart-ass comment back to everything that came out of my mouth. Noemi whipped us up and down the driveway in her two-seater Range Rover while I watched Maverick get his cardio workout in by jumping rope and taking jab after jab at his Everlast punching bag. Warmth spread across my chest as I watched him slide off his wife beater and toss it to the ground. My thighs instinctively clenched together as my insides melted to the floor into a puddle of sticky wet lust. All I could do was thank the heavens I had on shades because it was impossible to pry my eyes off him. Even if he wasn't my type, he was at least easy on the eyes, that was for sure.

When the battery on her truck began to die, Noemi pulled us back into the garage. I stole one more glance in his direction and saw a light-colored birthmark on his back shoulder in the shape of a large leaf.

"Enjoyin' the view?" he asked, turning to look at me without losing his count.

With a set of eight-pack abs and rippling muscles, resistible *he was not*. But I was wise enough not to let my heart surrender to what my body was beginning to crave.

"What?"

"Oh, I forgot. Your nigga look betta than me, right?"
He chuckled.

Instead of responding, I huffed and walked away. I
couldn't trust my own instincts around a shirtless Maverick
Malone. He needed to be clothed at all times in order for me
to think straight. I couldn't go out like that. I couldn't
become attracted to the one person I'd once loathed more
than anything.

Mav

I hated courtrooms. I hated judges and bailiffs, too.
But most of all, I was beginning to harbor hate for Suki's
mother. She was one of the first faces I recognized inside
the courtroom. I couldn't do shit but smile when the judge
ruled to keep Noemi in my custody until the next court date
in six months.

"This isn't the last you're going to see of me!"

"Noemi, say bye to your grandmother," I growled.

95

"Gammy will see you soon, baby girl, you can take that to the bank!" she said before storming off.

"I fuckin' hate that bitch," I grumbled.

River jabbed her elbow into my side. "Watch your mouth, that's still her grandmother."

"Whatever. Can you take her for a little while? I got some business I need to handle."

She frowned. "What do you have to do?"

"Why are you in my business? Can you take her or not?"

"I can, but you'll need to give me the car seat out of your car."

"Fine." I nodded. A nigga never pictured havin' a fuckin' car seat in the back of my whip or having to play pretend restaurant damn near every night.

ONCE RIVER AND NOEMI were on their way, I headed to meet with a new lawyer I was thinking about working with until the custody shit was behind me. I needed to know what I was truly up against. I was determined not to look like a fool in court and especially not in front of Suki's mother.

On the way, my phone rang, showing my boy Sosa's name on the screen. I was hoping he had good news for me.

Instead of wallowing in my grief, I buried myself into trying to figure out more details about Luca's death. I'd suffered the biggest loss my family had ever experienced. With my feelings of survivor's remorse at an all-time high, I wasn't going to rest until I knew the truth.

Sosa was part of my small inner circle. He, Luca, and I had spent years movin' weight up and down Spaghetti Junction. We'd seen a lot of niggas rise and fall, but he always stayed solid. Besides Luca, he was the only other nigga I trusted with my life.

"Yo," I answered.

"Sup, nigga."

I sighed. "Headed to meet with a lawyer about this custody shit. You?"

"Just picked up both my kids from their mother's crib. I got them for a couple days."

"Word, daddy duty and shit, I feel it."

"How's shit goin' under your roof?"

"Shit, you already know lil' shawty is givin' me a run for my money."

"Oh, for sure, but uh—listen, about what you asked me about…"

97

"Yeah?"

"I got some news you're gonna wanna hear," he said.

I tightened my grip on the steering wheel. "Aight, where you at? I'm about to pull up on you real quick."

"A nigga finna get a couple Happy Meals for the kids before I take 'em home. Pull up on me there, I'll drop a pin."

FIFTEEN MINUTES LATER, I pulled up beside Sosa's truck tucked away in a secluded parking spot. I got out of my car and hopped into his passenger seat. After dapping each other up, I looked at him. He was a dreaded hood nigga who wore glasses and was good as fuck with numbers.

"What did you have to tell me?"

He sighed. "Ain't nobody talkin' about your brother's accident, Mav. They're talking about you."

I frowned. "What?"

"You a high-profile nigga. Word on the street is when you got out, you wanted Luca out of the way to take back your rightful seat on the throne."

98

"What the fuck? If I wanted to be back in the game, I would be back in the fuckin' game. I told Luca I was out and that he could have everything. Why the fuck would I turn around and kill my own blood over something I ain't want?"

My body temperature shot up as my blood began to boil. The more I dug into what happened to my brother, the more I realized there was a target on my back. Somebody wanted both me and my brother out of the way completely. What better way than to kill one and let the other take the fall? Money, power, and influence were the only things niggas in the streets understood, which meant there was a price on my head.

He shrugged. "You know that, and I know that, but you know as well as I do, it only takes one pussy ass nigga to start some shit and then niggas gotta be put down."

"That's what just may need to be done then."

"There's something else."

"What?"

"I've been runnin' over the numbers, you know how I do. Everything's been in-sync up until after Luca died."

"You sayin' somethin' ain't right with the money?"

"I'm not sayin' anything yet until I know. I just wanted to put you on notice."

I nodded. "I gotta get to this meeting and shit. Let me know when you know somethin'."

As enraged as I was, it took everything in me to remain calm. Being anxious and rattled wasn't a good look. I needed more answers to know what I was really up against. Before I had the chance to formulate my next thought, my phone started to ring. I pulled it out of my pocket and saw River's name pop up on the screen.

I slid the phone up to my ear and answered. "Yeah."

"Meet me at the hospital!" she yelled.

My brows knitted in confusion. "What the fuck happened?"

"Noemi, she—she was jumping on the trampoline at the park, and she fell off and hurt her arm. She was crying like crazy, and I thought it might be broken so I didn't want to move her, so I called 9-1-1 and now we're in the back of the ambulance on the way to the hospital," she cried.

"Okay, just calm down and text me what hospital. I'm on my way," I told her.

Without saying another word, I hopped out of Sosa's passenger seat and back into my own whip. While sitting at the red light, I glanced over and saw a vacant building for sale. I had been on the hunt for available commercial property in the perimeter to open up my own tattoo shop.

Before the light turned, I snapped a picture of the real estate agent's information to reach out to her. I was finally ready to execute my exit plan now that I'd served my time, but as much as I wanted to be done with the streets, Sosa's news let me know that the streets weren't ready to be done with me.

The light turned green, and my phone pinged with River's text. I started on my way to check in on her and Noemi. All I could do was hope she was okay, and that River's overly sensitive ass was overreacting.

I DARTED THROUGH the emergency room doors and waited for River to come out and take me back to the room Noemi was in.

"How's she doing?"

River sighed. "She's okay. The doctor said it's just a sprain, thank God. I just feel so bad because she has to wear a cast for a week. I shouldn't have taken my eyes off her."

"Chill. You said it yourself she's fine, it's just a sprain. I'm sure the kid is tougher than she looks."

River nodded. "Yeah, she's taking it a lot better than I am. She thought riding in the ambulance was so cool."

I chuckled. "Yeah, you're a fuckin' wreck, and see, she's a Malone, she's tough as pig iron."

She snickered. "Shut up."

"But nah, I'm glad she's good though. You can't be callin' me all hysterical and shit like the world is about to end. You had me like damn, if a bullet don't take me out, I swear she'll be the death of me."

"You and me both. Come on, she's right in here."

"You alright, Kiddo?" I asked Noemi as I pulled back the curtain to her room.

She nodded. "Look at my cast! It's pink!"

"That's dope. Maybe later I'll draw you somethin' dope on there."

She smiled. "Okay."

"It doesn't even hurt that bad, right?"

"Nope."

"And you know what's the secret to makin' it heal faster?"

"What?"

"Ice cream."

"Yay!" she cheered.

River turned to look at me before we stepped off to the side to speak privately. "You're getting pretty good at this."

I shrugged. "Don't feel that way, but thanks."

"I'm serious, you are."

"I haven't done shit," I told her.

"Who got her dressed today?"

"She dressed herself for the most part."

"Okay, well, who got her fed today?"

"Chick-fil-A earlier today."

She sighed. "You know what I mean. All I'm saying is, it takes a village. You're doing your part, and I'm happy to help however I can."

"It doesn't take a village, it takes you."

She tilted her head to the side. "What do you mean?"

For the longest time I thought birds of a feather flocked together when it came to bitches like Suki. It wasn't until I got to know River that I realized that couldn't be further from the truth. It was crystal clear that I couldn't raise Noemi by myself, and her parents made sure I

103

wouldn't have to.

"I'm sayin' that you're all village Noemi needs, and I think you should move in with me—with us."

River

I'm sayin' that you're all village Noemi needs, and I think you should move in with me—with us.

His question kept replaying over and over in my head.

Living in his house?

Under his roof?

Being under one roof with Maverick for more than a few hours at a time was a thought that never entered even the smallest crevices of my mind.

"Move in?" I asked, his words pulling what was left of the rug right out from underneath my feet.

"I can't do this shit without you, River. We both know that."

I didn't know what the fuck to say. Being vulnerable was something I thought he was incapable of. "I—um…"

"Listen, I'm thinkin' strategically here. All we have to do is hold it down for six months, long enough for the court date. You can be my character witness to make sure Noemi stays where the fuck she should be, and that's with me and not with her grandparents. After that, you can move out, go wherever, whatever."

I sighed. As much as I loved children, a mother's love was something I could never replace or even duplicate. I loved spending time with Noemi, but day in and day out would be a big adjustment. Maverick and I both had big shoes to fill, but I wasn't sure we had to do it under one roof.

"Can I take some time to think about it?" I managed to mutter out.

He nodded. "Yeah, just hit me when you got an answer for me."

"Okay…"

BY THE TIME I got home, the last of my energy

106

had been depleted. I pulled my bags out of the car and headed up to my apartment. Just as I reached for my keys, I saw something taped onto my door.

"An eviction notice?!" I yelled, before quickly looking over my shoulder to make sure no one heard my outburst.

I quickly snatched the paper down and got inside to read over it. It turns out Leander hadn't been paying the rent for the past three months. He'd been taking my half of the rent money and pocketing it—all likely a part of his "great escape" breakup plan.

"Such a fuckin' coward!" I screamed as warms tears seeped down my cheeks.

I hated feeling weak! Even more, I hated that I was going from relying on one nigga to relying on another. That's not how I wanted it to be, but I was literally out of options. I didn't have three months of backpay to avoid getting evicted on top of trying to find extra coins for the rent increase. There was just no way I could afford it. I plopped down on the couch and glanced down at my phone. As much as I wanted to call Leander's ass until I couldn't call him anymore, I knew all that negative energy would be wasted. It was clear he didn't give a fuck about me and hadn't for some time. I looked down to see Maverick's name as the last person I called. As luck would have it, it seemed like I needed Noemi and Maverick as much as they needed me. Without taking a second longer to think, I quickly texted him my answer.

Me: [10:42pm]: My answer is yes.

 A WEEK LATER, the majority of my things were moved into a storage unit while the rest went to Maverick's house. I was still getting used to how much space there was. With over 4,000 square feet, there was more than enough room for the three of us. I was nervous that we were going to be living on top of each other, but Noemi and I slept in rooms upstairs, while the master suite was on the main level of his five-bedroom home.

 I had officially made it through the last day of school, and it was the first night I had time to myself, and I decided to try and cook dinner. I'd spent so much time moving after work and grabbing fast food on the go, that I hadn't taken the time to explore the kitchen. A part of me was curious to see what he had in his fridge. With my head buried inside, I was surprised to see that his minimalist décor vibes were also present in his eating habits. There were various flavors of vitamin water, mixed greens, fresh fruit, and almond milk inside. On top of the fridge were two different boxes of cereal—Honey Nut Cheerios for him, and Fruity Pebbles for her.

"You lookin' for somethin' in particular?" Mav asked, coming around the corner.

"Well, I was going to attempt to cook dinner, but uh…didn't see much to choose from in your fridge."

"What were you looking for?"

"I—I don't know, I was just trying to see what I could make out of what you have, but uh, from the looks of it, we're either having fruit salad or cereal."

"Text me whatever you want, and I'll have Rosa go shopping in the morning."

"Rosa?" I asked.

"The housekeeper."

"I thought her name was uh…Florence?"

"That's the gardener," he corrected me.

"Pardon me, your liege. I forgot I was living amongst royalty," I said, before curtseying in front of him.

"Knock it off," he said, walking into the living room.

I'd grown bored of rummaging through his kitchen and leaned over the island to jot down a few groceries the house needed. I looked out of the kitchen window over the sink, getting a nice view of the private, wooded backyard with a fire pit. He didn't look like the type to entertain too much company, but he was definitely prepared to. I turned my attention to the giggles coming from the living room and walked in to see Noemi and Mav sitting on the floor with their heads underneath a comforter.

"What are y'all doing?" I asked.

"Shh! We're in a secret club," Noemi whispered, poking her head out from underneath the cover.

"Well, I need to speak to your Uncle Mav really quick."

"He can't talk. He's busy."

"Busy doing what? I can see him right there," I said, pointing to the oversized blob underneath the cover.

"You can't talk to him unless you're in the club."

"But if I'm not in the club, how can I talk to you?" I quizzed.

"Because I'm the princess."

She stated her words loud and clear as if they'd been scribed in the rule book that I'd forgotten to read. "Well, can I be in your secret club?"

"Umm…"

"Pleaseeeeee?" I asked, poking out my lip.

"It's very, very exclusive."

"Yeah, top fuckin' secret," he added.

I laughed. "Pleaseeeeee? I've always wanted to be in a secret club! Plus…I wanted to order pizza for dinner, and it'll be a real shame if I have to eat it all by myself."

"Okay, fine, but you have to say the password."

"What's the password?" I whispered.

"Needle nose panty pinchers," she whispered in my ear.

I burst out laughing. "I'm sorry, needle what?"

"You have to say it to be in the club!"

"Uh, okay…needle nose panty pinchers?" I said with uncertainty in my voice.

"Welcome to the secret club!"

By the time Noemi, Mav, and I ate pizza, played games, and watched *Frozen 1* and *2* back-to-back, she was practically falling asleep where she stood.

111

"I think it's about time somebody goes to bed," I whispered.

"I'll carry her up, and you tuck her in," he told me.

"Okay." I nodded.

I followed behind him as he cradled Noemi's sleeping body in his strong arms. Warmth began to spread across my chest again, and I grabbed onto the railing. The coolness of the steel railing began to bring me back to myself. I was just so impressed at how attentive he was with her. It was almost as if anything outside of these walls didn't matter. For someone as well-known as he was, I was sure he was a hot commodity in many people's lives, but not once did he even try to drag his attention away from her. I went to bed thinking maybe he really wasn't so bad after all.

MY EYES OPENED before the sun had even cracked the sky. I rolled over to see what time it was and groaned at the 2:30 a.m. staring back at me. I tossed and turned for fifteen more minutes before I decided that sleep was no longer going to come to me if I kept chasing it. My socks sailed forth down the stairs and against the slick kitchen floor covered in marble. I stopped dead in my tracks when I saw a shirtless Maverick sitting at the eat-in kitchen table with his back to me.

"Hey, I uh—I can't sleep, do you have any tea?"

"Check the pantry," he said, peering at me over his shoulder.

112

"Do you want a cup?"

"Nah, I'm good with what I got right here."

I stepped a little closer and noticed the bottle of Henny, three rolled blunts, and weed on the table. "Oh," I said before stationing myself in the corner of the kitchen while I waited for the water to heat up. "Why aren't you sleep?"

"I'm a night owl."

"Then when do you sleep? Because you're clearly up in the daytime, too."

"You ever hear somebody say that sleep is the cousin to death? So, it's not one of my favorite pastimes," he said, slipping a blunt between his lips.

After just two puffs, weed smoke filled the air. "You know how to roll?" he asked.

I quickly shook my head. "No."

"Watch me then."

"Don't you think you have enough rolled?"

"You wanna learn or not?"

I frowned. As bad as I wanted to tell him that I'd survive without having that skillset under my belt, I walked

113

over quietly and watched him.

"I'ma show you how to roll the perfect blunt," he boasted.

I stood beside him with my arms folded. The longer I watched, the more captivated I became. He tore open the Dutch wrapper with his teeth and split the blunt open with precision.

I watched him pull out a large nugget of weed and smile. "Look at it, isn't it gorgeous?"

I grimaced. "Is that the *Blue Dream* again or whatever you called that death sentence you were smoking the last time?"

"That gas." He smiled before grinding his weed up.

Mav lined the inside of the blunt with as much weed as he could, pressed it all in, and the licked it across to seal it. The way his long tongue slid up and down the blunt had me completely mesmerized. I shifted one leg in front of the other and immediately began doing Kegels. That coupled with the fact that I was standing next to his warm, shirtless body had my mind spinning.

"All done."

"Thanks for the lesson," I told him before walking back over to finish making my tea.

114

"What's got you up this late? Since you been here, you been goin' to bed at like 9:30."

"Why you clockin' me?" I retorted.

He scoffed. "I'm not. I just didn't know you and Noemi had the same bedtime." He chuckled.

I huffed. "Whatever."

"What? You had a bad day or somethin'?"

"Last day, thank God."

"Shit, you look like you need a drink."

"That's why I got my tea."

He grabbed the bottle of Henny off the table before pulling himself to his feet. "Take a shot with me," he said, sliding the bottle across the island to me.

My hands flew up in protest. "Wait, what? I came down here for tea, that's it and that's all."

He smiled a lopsided grin. "Oh, you scared? Is that it?"

"You're trying to taunt me like a little schoolboy, and I'm not fallin' for it."

"Fine, fuck it. I'll drink by myself," he said, pouring

himself a glass.

I raised my chin until my eyes met his. He was staring me down while washing down his first shot with another. I rolled my eyes. He was not going to paint me out to be some timid schoolgirl who backed away from a challenge. I'd just had one of the longest and most frustrating days of my entire career, and I still made the conscious effort to leave all that shit at the door and not bring it into the house. If anybody deserved to get shit faced, it was me.

"You know what? Fuck it! Give me a glass."

"Please."

I sucked my teeth. "Please?" I asked, with all types of attitude bouncing around in my tone.

Mav passed me a glass, and I poured a small amount into my cup. "You ain't gon' feel nothin' from that lil' drop your ass just poured."

"Shut up! Do you want to hear about my day or not?"

"Not really."

"Oh!" I could feel my skin heating up with embarrassment.

116

"Nah, I'm kiddin', tell me what happened to knock you off your square."

I took a swig of the Henny and squinted my eyes as the liquor set my insides ablaze. I should've just stuck with the fuckin' tea. "So today was the last day of school, right, and I had to pass all of my kids after strongly recommending to my principal that at least three of them be held back. They just don't have a good grasp of the skills and know-how to be successful in the next grade. Despite my best efforts—I mean, I changed my teaching methods, I tutored them afterschool. I tried to hold parent-teacher conferences that *none* of their fuckin' parents showed up to!"

"They asses can't go to summer school?" he asked.

"Summer school isn't enough, but they made me pass them along because we don't have the fuckin' funding to pay teachers to teach this summer, so they have to keep the amount of kids small to spread amongst the teachers they can afford to pay. I fuckin' hate this school system! Always wanna talk about no child left behind when they willingly let kids fall through the cracks because of money. People wanna talk about how we're the greatest fuckin' country in the world and yet we can't spare money for something as important as fuckin' education! It's ridiculous!"

"You know what else is ridiculous? It's this increasing pressure that everybody feels from the top down.

117

All they care about are good, standardized test scores. They don't really give a fuck about these kids. The ones in the classroom with them every day, we're the ones who care. And who do they pay the least as if we don't bend over backwards to teach America's children—us! Fuckin' teachers! I'm sorry—rant over!" I huffed.

He chuckled. "Goddamn, shawty."

I shrugged. "I'm sorry, I don't have anybody to talk to besides a five-year-old who doesn't understand. It's nice to have an actual conversation with an adult."

"Why don't you talk to your man about it?"

I rolled my eyes, forgetting how big of a deal I'd made about having a man that I no longer actually had. "About that…"

"You ain't gotta explain shit to me. I been knew you was cappin'."

"Excuse me?"

"Ain't no man in his right mind gon' let his bitch— I'm sorry, his woman live under the same roof as a nigga like me and be cool with it. If he is, he a fool and you don't need to be in the presence of that mothafucka anyway."

"I was in a relationship, it just ended abruptly as fuck, to be honest. When you were all in my space at the party, I was still tryna process everything and maybe I laid it on a little too thick," I admitted.

"A little?" He chuckled. "You had me thinkin' that nigga was about to pop up on me or somethin' for sayin' hello to you."

A smile crept across my face. "Yeah, er. Sorry about that. It's uh, it's over now. It's just me."

"It's better that way."

I scoffed. "Speak for yourself."

He nodded. "I am."

Here we go again with this macho bullshit, I thought to myself. "…He broke up with me through text, you know? And then blocked me."

Mav's eyes lit up in shock before he scowled. "Pussy."

I shook my head. "I guess the signs were there, I don't know. Maybe they weren't, but I guess I'll never know now."

"You shouldn't need to know. You dodged a bullet with that nigga. You already got your own pussy, why you need to be with a nigga with another?"

I was speechless. Mav's directness struck a chord in

119

me. Whether good or bad was to be determined.

"But I'm probably not the one you should be taking relationship advice from since I'ma a suede-intellect, or whatever the fuck that college shit you said to me before."

"It's pseudo-intellectual, but yeah…"

"Luca told me you were a teacher and shit, what made you want to get into teaching in the first place?"

"I wanna make a difference. I just didn't think it would be this hard."

"That's real, but nothin' easy is ever worth it."

I cracked a slight smile. "I guess you're right."

"I know I am."

"Well, thanks for the drink…and the talk."

"Goodnight, River."

"Goodnight."

SEVEN

Mav

I was sitting in my private office counting the stacks of money inside my built-in safe when my phone rang. It was the realtor calling me back about the building I'd seen as a potential location for my tattoo shop. With the money I'd invested into the stock market and put away for my exit plan, plus the money Luca funneled my way from the streets while I was tucked away, I had more than enough capital to open a successful business. All I needed was the building.

"Hello?" I answered.

"Hi, is this Mr. Malone?"

"Yeah."

"Hello, this is Lauren Combs calling you back. You left a message about the property on—"

"Yeah," I said, cutting her off, "is the property still available?"

"It actually went under contract as of this morning, but I do have a few other commercial properties across the city I could show you, just tell me what you're looking for."

"Yeah, I'll send you some information on what I'm looking for, and when you got somethin' to show me, we'll find some time to link."

"Sounds good, I look forward to doing business with you," she said before ending the call.

I ended the call when I heard a faint knock on my door. I quickly closed the safe and gave the dial a hard spin. I walked over to the door and locked eyes with Noemi.

"What's up?" I asked.

"Me and Auntie River need pillows…"

"*AND BLANKETS!*" River yelled from upstairs.

"Yeah, and blankets."

I screwed up my forehead. "What you need all that for?"

"We're making a fort!"

I shook my head. River wasn't shit but a pretty ass,

big ass kid, which made for the perfect companion for Noemi. "Upstairs in the hallway, you'll find everything you need."

"Okay!"

"Hold up, what do you say?"

"Oh, uh thank you!" she squealed before scurrying away.

I MADE MY WAY upstairs to the kitchen and was stopped by Noemi. "Look what we made, Uncle Mav! Do you like it?"

"Yeah, do you like our fort?" River asked, playing along.

"Not really."

"Excuse me."

"You heard me."

She scoffed. "Oh, like you could do better."

"Actually, I can. You set the bar pretty low."

She effortlessly rolled her eyes, making sure I saw it before zeroing in on my left arm. "Is that new?" she asked, pointing to the tattoo of Noemi's name on my wrist.

"What? This?" I asked. I was surprised she noticed it in the sea of ink on my body.

"Yeah, I did it a few days ago."

"Hold up, you did your own tattoo? Like tattooed it into your own skin?"

I nodded. "Yeah."

"You're licensed?"

"Not yet, that's the goal though, well, the goal is really to open my own tattoo shop, and once it's open, I'll bring in master tattooists and expand my craft under them. I own the shit, but I also get to learn from the best and get my license after that."

The look on her face told me she was surprised that I had a game plan that didn't involve movin' weight.

"Wow…I know you have a lot of tats, but I didn't know you took tattoos so seriously."

"Tattooing is more than just needles and ink. It's art. It's expression. It's freedom. You got any tats?"

"No."

"I think everybody should have at least one custom thing tatted on them."

"Why is that?" she quizzed.

"Because not one single mothafucka on this earth is like the other. We may all breathe the same air, but we're all different."

I was a lover of art in unusual forms and felt like all tattoos were personally meaningful art pieces. Tattooing was the only thing that satisfied my creative needs.

"I definitely don't have a high pain tolerance to sit through getting a tattoo without squealing," she admitted.

"You can't take a lil' pain?"

"Absolutely not, you're gonna have to give me a few shots to get me in your chair."

Before I had the chance to respond, she turned her attention to her phone. "It's her uh...*G-A-M-M-Y*."

I scowled. "What the fuck does she want?"

"She wants me to talk to you about letting them see her for the weekend."

"That's simple, no."

She shook her head. "Look, I get it, but—"

"I said no!" I growled and walked back into the kitchen.

125

She quickly followed behind me. "Why not?"

"So, she can fill her head up with bullshit about me? Hell no, fuck that bitch with a sick dick," I said.

"Don't be petty, Mav. It's a test."

"Test or not, I don't bend for nobody."

"Nobody except Noemi, and whether you like it or not, that's the closest thing to having a piece of Suki around as she'll get. She needs that."

"No she don't, she got you."

Her brow furrowed as she looked at me sternly. "Mav—"

"Fine. Set it up."

River

THE IRIDESCENT BUBBLES floated on top of the warm bath water as I swirled my fingertips inside to check the temperature. All I wanted to do for the rest of the evening was soak in the tub until I was a life-sized prune and then lay my naked body against the high thread count sheets. Just as I was about to get undressed, I heard a strong knock on my bedroom door. I scurried over to the door, forgetting to refasten my pants and swung open the door to see Mav staring back at me.

"Yo, I'm about to take Noemi out for some ice cream before she leaves this weekend. You wanna ride?" he asked.

As surprised as I was that he'd thought far enough to invite me, I declined. "Nah, I'm not gonna go. You two have fun together."

"You sure?" he asked, his six-foot-three frame towering over me.

"Yeah, I think I'll take this alone time to do some self-care, y'know? Take a bath, binge watch a season of some show or something."

He smirked and looked down at my unbuttoned pants. "Yeah, aight. Don't flick the bean too hard."

My forehead crinkled. "What?"

"You'll get it when you get it," he said before walking away.

I LET MY NAKED BODY submerge under the pressure of the warm, soapy bath water as Sade's sultry

127

voice rang through my iPhone speaker. I sang the lyrics alongside her to one of my favorite songs, *The Sweetest Taboo*. As the song came to a close, I closed my eyes and an image of none other than Maverick Malone popped into my mind, followed by another, and then several more. From his smile, to his shirtless body and muscles, to the dick print I was sure I'd seen on occasion, all reason had fled as my fantasies formed mirages of him and I in my mind.

Next thing I knew, I found my hand in between my thighs while the other ran over my nipples. The moment I touched my clit, I heard Mav's voice loud and clear in my head, *Yeah, aight. Don't flick the bean too hard.* I shot up, letting his words form meaning in my head. He was talking about masturbating. I wouldn't give him the satisfaction of being right, but it was clear my body was calling out for some sexual attention, and I wanted it from him. He was a magnetic force that was just too powerful to ignore. Every time we're in the same room, I felt it pulling at my sanity and my self-control.

Mav

The first thing I noticed when River swung open her door was that she had on red lipstick. *Fuck.* Red was my favorite color and something I loved to see a woman in. For the rest of the short conversation, all I could do was stare at her full, juicy bottom lip. I wanted to bite the fuck out of it. Before she even got a chance to say a word, I lifted her chin and brought her lips to mine. I gently slid my hands up the sides of her neck and up to the sides of her face. The kiss intensified as I slipped my tongue inside her mouth and heard her moan. Her small hands rested on top of mine, and I could feel my dick starting to stiffen.

I pulled away from her, and she flashed her eyes up at me. "Mav—" she whispered, trying to bring her heartrate back down.

"I'm sorry. I don't even kiss like that."

"Then why'd you just kiss me?" she asked, gently brushing the side of her hand past her bottom lip.

"You looked too damn good not to…" I admitted before walking away.

I can't have her.

I won't have her, I repeated to myself as I walked down the stairs.

Before asking her to move in to help with Noemi, I promised myself I wouldn't touch her. I wasn't one to shit where I ate, and I knew doing anything with her would eventually make for a hostile household. I wasn't about to have drama underneath the same roof where I laid my head at night.

The next day.

"Hey, um I'm getting ready to take Noemi to Suki's parents for the weekend and since I'll be there, I'm going to just stay the weekend with my parents, and we'll be back on Sunday," River announced.

I nodded. "Yeah, aight. Just let me know what you need."

"Well, you could tell me what last night was about...*and* you could let me take the G-Wagon."

I chuckled. She was out of her rabbit ass mind. "You can take the S-Class. I'll never let you drive my wagon," I said, handing her the keys to my matte gray Mercedes.

"And about last night?"

"What about it?" I asked, biting down on my bottom lip.

She stared at me for a few seconds before rolling her eyes. "Fine, that's the one I really wanted anyway." She chuckled and winked at me.

WITH BOTH NOEMI and River out of the house, I could clear my head. I welcomed the space and alone time to put the focus back on my business as I sat in my living room talking to the real estate agent face-to-face. Her picture on that sign didn't do her justice. Shawty had curves in all of the right places and a beautiful face to match. It also didn't hurt that she came through drippin' in a red Prada suit either.

"So, you say you're looking to open a tattoo shop, so of course you want prime locations to bring in lots of traffic. Somewhere that street parking is available, so nobody gets a ticket while their getting tatted." She chuckled, blessing my eyes with her pretty white teeth.

"Exactly."

"So based on that, plus the information you've already sent me about your preferences, I have three properties available right now to show you all within the price point you set."

I nodded. "That's exactly what I wanted to hear."

"Never worry, Mr. Malone. I do my job and I do it very well, but I must ask, exactly how far into the process have you gotten? I mean, do you have a business license? Will you be able to obtain all the permits you need on time? I ask because I work with top dollar clients who have the means and the know-how and are ready to jump when I show them exactly what they want. By the looks of your home, I can see you're r—"

"Ready to do business," I said, changing the course of her sentence.

I couldn't be mad at her for not wanting to waste her time, but I was ready with cash in hand.

She smiled once more. "Great, so am I. So, I have another showing in about an hour, but if you have some time over the next couple of days we can maybe get together, and I can show you the three locations. Based off them, you tell me what you want, and I'll make it happen. I've got connections all over the city."

"Connections, I like that."

"I thought you would."

"Bet, just text me when and where, and I'll be there."

WHEN SATURDAY ROLLED around, I woke up to an empty house and a text message from Lauren with a time and a location. I smiled and began to start my day. Three hours later, she and I had been all over the city and seen the three locations she promised.

"So, now that you've seen all three, what do you think?"

132

"I definitely like the second one, gives us room to grow and everybody doesn't have to be all on top of each other."

"I agree, and there's always available parking around the area and it's not even a block away from a public transit stop."

"Let's do it then. I've got cash in hand ready to go."

She flashed her bright smile my way. "Perfect, let me make some calls and get some paperwork drawn up, and I'll definitely be in touch."

"Yo, your smile is pretty as shit," I complimented her.

"Thank you," she grinned, "yours is really nice, too."

"Thanks. You've made this process as stress free as possible for me so far, and I appreciate that shit."

"As your realtor, it's my job to alleviate your stress. I'm always ready to *put in work*," she said, glancing up at me.

Neither of us were speaking, but her eyes were telling me everything I needed to hear. "Word, I'ma have to change your name to *Stress Reliever* in my phone."

"Call me anytime, and I got you."

LATER THAT NIGHT, I was sitting in my office with my phone on speaker, listening to Sosa talk.

"Did you get a name yet?"

"Nothin' solid yet, but don't worry, somethin' will come. It always does."

I huffed. "Yeah, aight, bet. Just let me know somethin' the moment you know somethin'."

"What you gon' do about the business? You gon' have to make your next move sooner than later."

"I'm about to play my card in a minute, don't worry about that, but as far as the streets go, I got a long hand on things and that's how it needs to stay for now. I want to be lowkey on how I move until I get more answers about who the fuck is talkin' and what really happened to my brother."

"I got you."

I hung up and my fingertips were drawn to my temples like magnets. I'd gone from having a stress-free day to being wound up and agitated. I scrolled down my contacts and hit the name *Stress Reliever* in my phone to text Lauren. I knew better than to mix business with pleasure, but River was off limits, and I needed the release.

Me: [11:42pm]: "You say you a stress reliever,

right? I'm tryna see what that's about."

AN HOUR LATER, I was sitting in the living room with my arms pressed behind my head and my topless real estate agent in between my legs.

"I was happy when you hit me up," she admitted while gripping my dick with both hands.

"Shh, just suck on the head," I instructed her.

I didn't call her over to talk. I wanted her to do what she said she could do, relieve my stress. She sucked and whipped her tongue around the head a few times before dropping lower on her knees to put my balls in her mouth. She pushed her hair behind her ears and started to spit on my dick like her ass was beatboxing.

"Yeah, that's it, spit on it. Get that dick nice and wet."

She indulged me and began to drop so much spit on the head that she made it squeak between her lips

"Mmm, shit. You like the way it taste, don't you?" I asked, feeding more of my dick down her throat.

She nodded while flicking her tongue across the tip before deep throating me so good, my eyes started to roll in the back of my head.

I palmed the back of her head, pushing her as low onto my dick as her throat would allow. "Ooooh shit."

As good as the head felt, I had to know what the pussy felt like. I stood up and led her down the hallway to my bedroom.

"Get in here and bend that ass over…"

I WOKE UP MAD at the world that she was still lying next to me. I'd fucked around at let her spend the night.

"Yo, wake up," I mumbled, stirring her from her sleep. "I don't do sleepovers."

She shot up and began bobbing her head. "No, it's cool. Me either, especially not with clients. I literally never, ever do this, but I could hear the *D* callin' me through your pants, and I just had to ride it one time. Trust me, this will not change our working relationship!" she said, all while getting redressed and swiping up her Christian Louboutin heels in her hand.

I nodded. She'd said exactly what I wanted to hear. Had she said anything but, we'd be having a completely different conversation.

"I will say though, for someone who was just so…*giving* a few hours ago, you sure are icy now."

"It's not you. I just don't make it a habit of bringing people into my space, and on the rare occasion that I do, they never spend the night."

Her perfectly arched eyebrows perked up. "Oh, okay, trust issues, got it."

"You'd have 'em too if niggas was sayin' you killed your own flesh and blood."

She stopped for a second and tilted her head to the side as if she was running plays through her mind. "Wait…oh shit. That was *your* brother? I remember hearing something about that. Was it a car crash or something?"

"What exactly did you hear?" I pressed.

She shook her head. "No, nothing. I'm sorry, I shouldn't have said anything. I know it's a tough subject for you and I don't want to make anything worse."

"What did you hear?" I asked again.

"I heard exactly what you said. I was out at Club Mirage with a couple of my girlfriends a few weeks ago, no names or anything, just that a someone died and it didn't seem like so much of an accident, if you know what I mean."

"And did you believe it?"

She shrugged. "It doesn't matter what I believe. I

137

wasn't there, so I'll never know. No one will."

"Had you known it was me they were talking about before we started working together, would you have done business with me?"

"To be honest, if the money is right, I'll damn near work with anyone," she admitted.

I nodded while pulling on some basketball shorts to see her ass out. She'd given me all the information I needed to know. She boasted about her connections, and I wanted to know just how good they were. Just as my hand hit the front door knob, I heard a car door slam outside. *Fuck,* I thought. River and Noemi had come back way earlier than I expected. I opened the door, and River greeted me with a smile.

"Hey—back early, I know, but my parents were really starting to get on my fuc—" she paused when she saw Lauren standing behind me with her keys and shoes in hand.

Before I got the chance to say anything, Noemi ran up beside her. "Who is that?" she asked, eyeing Lauren.

"C'mon and let's go get your stuff out of the car, Noemi, and let Uncle Mav say bye to his *friend.*"

Once River and Noemi were back at the car, Lauren slipped past and left. Noemi ran back inside, and River brushed past me without saying a word.

138

"River."

"Unbelievable!" she whispered until Noemi was out of earshot.

"It wasn't the plan for her to spend the night, and I didn't expect for y'all to get back so early," I admitted.

"I didn't know we were cramping your style. No, better yet, I didn't even know we were on that type of time, bringing randoms into the house where Noemi lays her head? But go off, Mav. You got it."

"I'm grown ass man, River. I'm not gon' apologize for gettin' pussy in my own house," I reminded her.

"You right! It is your house, so do whatever the fuck you want. See if I give a fuck!"

She whipped her neck with sass and walked away.

As cool as she was trying to play it, we both knew better. I could see the hurt in her eyes. She needed to know that we would never be on that level. I just couldn't afford to give any female a part of me outside of Noemi. All my focus had to be on her well-being, and for that to happen, I needed to do two things: open the shop and get back to the streets to really find out what I'd been missing.

EIGHT

Mav

Seeing River switch between moping around the house one minute to giving me the cold shoulder the next had me feeling a way. Since our last awkward encounter and argument, she hadn't said more than two words to me in a couple of weeks. Yet, I'd just finalized the process of buying my first piece of commercial property, and I wanted to celebrate. Against my better judgment, I went upstairs and knocked on her door.

"Ride with me," I said as soon as she opened the door.

"For what?"

"Just c'mon."

"Are you going to tell me where we're going?"

"Why does it matter?"

"Stop answering my question with a question and just tell me so I know what to put on," she said, followed by an eye roll.

"Stop thinking so much, and just throw on something red. Be ready in fifteen."

RIVER TOSSED HER body in my passenger seat wearing a black crop top, gray sweatpants, a pair of high-top Vans on her feet, and a set of kissable lips painted candy apple red. My dick throbbed in my joggers. I wanted to kiss more than just her first set of lips. Shawty looked good enough to eat.

"Nice lips," I told her.

She shrugged. "You said wear something red, so…"

"Nah, it looks good. It's my favorite color, and I love to see a woman in it."

"Oh…so now that you've got me in the car, you gon' tell me where we goin'?" she asked.

"You'll see when we get there."

We rode under the clear sapphire skies, passing by various *Keep Georgia Clean* street signs and strip maps filled with Korean and Black-owned businesses. Twenty minutes later, we pulled up across the street from an empty store front, and I put the truck in park.

"Are we here?" she asked.

"Yup."

"What is this place?"

"It's my tattoo shop."

Her eyes widened. "Oh shit. For real?"

I held up the keys and jingled them in her face. "For real."

"When did this happen?"

"Earlier today. You're the only person who knows."

She flashed me a smile. It was the warmest things she'd sent my way in weeks. River's smiles were always warm and inviting like home and easily the first thing I noticed about her.

"Can we go in?"

"That's why I brought you here. Let's go."

We walked inside, and I turned on the light to illuminate the blank space. When I looked around, I saw a blank canvas that I was about to unleash my creative mind and artistic skills on to make it custom.

"Wow, it's pretty spacious in here. That's good for privacy," River commented.

"You got a name for it?"

"M3 Ink, for my name, Maverick Muhammad Malone."

She bobbed her head in approval. "Nice. How long you think it's gonna take you to finish it all?"

"I don't know for real. There's a lot of shit I gotta do like permits and inspections, furniture, design, security systems…it's a lot, but I'ma get it done as soon as I can to get this shit off the ground. It's been a long time comin' and I ain't come this far just to play pussy now. I ain't got time to be unsuccessful."

"No, I think this is all really great. I'll be happy when you do open up. This is big, and if no one else tells you, congratulations, you're officially a business owner."

I smiled. She didn't know I owned shares in dozens of the companies that produced the products she consumed on a daily basis, but that was a conversation for another day. "Thanks. I was thinkin' I do a whole mural over on that wall so that it's visible from the street, make a nigga wanna come in and get inked, you know? And then maybe I do another one on the ground since its concrete."

"Yeah, that would be dope, like a custom welcome mat. What were you thinking as far as like furniture for your waiting area?"

"Haven't gotten that far yet. You got any suggestions?"

"Well, whatever you choose, I think it should mimic the minimalist vibe at the house, but like with a pop of color, like that mural you plan to create."

I nodded, impressed with how much thought she put behind her input on the spot. "I like that. Maybe something black, it's sleek—sexy."

"Black leather. White is going to make you want to wish you were never born."

"Shit, you should just design the shit for me."

She giggled. "I am pretty good at this, ain't I? Just make sure I'm one of the first people you tat when you get your license."

"Since when you change your mind about wanting a tat? Last I checked you were too chicken shit."

"Oh, don't get it twisted, I'm still all the way nervous. I'd need like three shots of tequila to get up enough courage to sit in your chair."

I've got something else your ass can sit on, I thought to myself. The more she talked, the more I zeroed in on her bright red lips. Instead, I responded with a nod. "I got a bottle of Henny in the back."

"I thought you said you just got the keys today."

"I got them earlier, and the realtor gave me a lil' shop-warming basket with a bunch of shit in it, a bottle of Henny being one of them."

"I didn't expect to be drinking on an empty stomach. You gon' have to break this pretty young thang off with a meal first, playboy," she joked.

"Sounds like you scared to me."

"I'm not."

144

"Sure sounds like it," I repeated.

"Whatever. One, Maverick Muhammad Malone. One shot!" she declared.

Say my fuckin' name again, I said to myself. It was taking everything in me not to lose control, but a nigga was slippin' through the cracks second by second. She followed me to the back and watched me crack open the bottle. I turned it up to my lips for a few gulps before passing it to her. She frowned and pushed it away. "What? You scared to drink after me or somethin'?"

She turned down her lips. "Boy, I don't know where your mouth has been."

Shit, I know where it could be, I muttered deep in my private thoughts.

"Question."

"Answer," I responded.

"Why'd you tell me first?"

"You're the only one I wanted to tell," I admitted.

"Why me?"

"I don't know, maybe I liked it better when you were talkin' my fuckin' head off every day instead of givin' me the cold shoulder."

She rolled her eyes. "Give me the damn bottle."

"Oh, you takin' the shot now?" I teased.

"Only because you were honest," she said, before tossing her head back and taking a swig straight with no chaser. She instantly gripped her chest as if she was having a heart attack and sat the bottle down with a thud. "There, you got, the one shot I said I would do."

145

"Yeah, aight. And for the record, I'm always honest."

She scoffed. "Only when it benefits you."

"Pass me the bottle," I said, changing the subject.

"I'm not your maid. Come over here and get it yourself."

I smirked at the sexy little sasshole that she was and made sure to brush up against her when I grabbed it. "My fault."

She smacked her lips. "Watch where you're going," she retorted.

"What was that?" I asked, shamelessly slipping my arms around her waist and letting my lips brush against the nape of her neck. "You smell good as shit by the way."

She shivered before turning her head to the side. "Stop, that tickles…"

"If you want me to move, then tell me to move."

"But what if I don't?" she asked innocently.

"I promised myself I wouldn't touch you…but *fuck it*. I at least have to taste those lips…"

Our lips brushed against each other a few times, breath fanning across each other's faces as we waited for the other to make the next move. I held back for a few

146

seconds to make sure she was comfortable before I started kissing and licking her neck. Soon, I felt her body jolt and quake in my arms. I'd found her sweet spot. I finally had her in my grasp, and I was ready to toss every last ounce of my self-control out the window. I scooped her up in my arms and sat her body on top of the counter.

With her back parallel to the cold countertop, I started pulling down her pants and red laced panties. "Fuck," I said, biting my lip.

I pressed my thumb against her clit, rubbing it slowly through her panties. "I wanna tease it for a little. Is that alright with you?"

"Mmm, yeah. Rub it nice and slow just like that," she said, chewing her bottom lip.

After I'd managed to make her form a wet spot in the seat of her panties, I pulled them completely off, ready to taste the most forbidden fruit. I pressed her knees back toward her face before I buried my tongue deep inside her. My lips and tongue took turns sucking and flicking her pulsating clit.

"Ooooh shiiiiiiiittttttt," she hissed, locking her arms underneath her legs and looking down at me. I flattened my tongue against her clit while staring deep into her eyes.

"Yeah, hold those legs back for me," I said, licking up her slit and sinking my fingertips into her ass cheeks.

147

River gripped the back of my head as I caressed her folds with my tongue. "Mmm, yeah. Shit, I'm about to—I—I!" she squealed.

My lips continued to glide back and forth against her pussy until her body quaked and quivered. Watching River's juices drip down the crack of her ass was the sexiest shit I'd ever seen. My dick was throbbing so much it was starting to hurt. Before things went to the next level, I ripped my lips away from her body and stood to my feet with my dick print bulging through my pants. I knew no nigga in his right mind would walk away from a situation like that, but I was trying to protect her. She didn't want it with me. A nigga like me couldn't be handled. All I would do was break her heart.

"I need to take you home," I told her.

She sprang up as if my voice was an alarm clock. "What? Now? No. What you need to do is finish what you started."

"Put your clothes back on, River. I'll meet you at the car," I said, before swiping the bottle of Henny into my grasp and walking out of the back room.

River

Seconds of silence faded between us on the excruciatingly long ride home. I was a flustered, horny, and hopeless ass mess. How could he bring me that far and not give me the dick? The more I stewed in my thoughts, the more enraged I became. Not mad because of what had just went down, but mad because it was bone-chillingly good, and I wanted more! Both my life and my body had been ambushed by the man. He was such a fuckin' poet the way his lips whispered sweet nothings and his tongue snaked over my juicy folds. If he could make me cum in less than ten minutes with just his mouth, I couldn't wait to see what his dick would do. I needed every inch of it. Before Mav left me, I could see the print of his hard dick curved halfway up his stomach which told me he wanted me just as bad. He was holding back, and I wanted to know why.

As soon as he killed the engine, I hopped out of the car and darted into the house.

"Yo, River, wait up," I heard him call out behind me.

I quickly whipped my neck around. "What?" I snapped.

I could see the depths of his waves underneath the moonlight as he stared at me blankly while chewing the inside of his lip. "I want you, River. I just—" his sentence trailing off into nothingness.

"What's stopping you?" I asked. I was practically standing in front of him ready and willing and he was letting the moment pass by.

"I promised myself I wouldn't," he stated.

"Why not? Is it because of Suki—or—"

He waved his hand in the air, causing me to pause the rest of my sentence. "It's none of that, I just know how shit like this ends."

"I've been thinking about that kiss every night since it happened," I admitted. "Do you know how hard it's been to be around you every day and act as if it never happened? Then seeing you with that other girl right after and now the shop…I just…"

"You wanna talk about hard? Imagine stifling this hard ass dick every day because I know I can't have you like I want to. Shit, knowing I can't press your body against that wall right now and give you this dick until you cry tears of joy for me," he said, gritting his teeth.

My knees quivered. The sound of his voice alone lubricated my flower. If he wanted me, he had one hell of a way of showing it. "Then come finish what you started."

He stepped into my space and slowly ran his thumb down my lips. "Say it again."

"Which part?"

"I wanna hear you say it again."

150

Instead of repeating myself verbatim, I said what was really on my mind, just dying to fall off the tip of my tongue. "I want you to fuck me, Mav."

His fingertips grazed the small of my back as his lips fused and held tight against mine. His tongue teased my lips apart while his hands raced down my waist and cradled my ass. He lifted my body up, and I entangled my legs around his waist. He carried us to his room, and I could feel his engorged dick pressing through his clothes. After laying me down on his bed, his large hands explored my breasts, massaging them and tugging at my nipples. I pulled my shirt over my head as he pulled my pants down to see I didn't have on any panties.

He smirked. "Oh, you just knew you were gettin' some dick tonight, huh?"

"They were soaking wet, so I left you something to remember me by at your shop," I replied.

"Soaking wet, huh?"

"Yeah."

"Let me see if I can get it wetter than before," he said before flipping me over on all fours and eating my pussy from behind.

With my ass up and face down, Mav started sucking on my pussy lips before slicing them open with his tongue. The low groaning and humming he was doing against my clit sent me into a frenzy.

151

"Mmm, pussy so sweet," he said, before lightly flickering his tongue against my clit. Mav tossed my cheeks between the palms of his hands. "Tell me what you want tonight."

"You."

"What about me?"

"Mmm shit. Your dick…mmm, deep…inside me," I panted, grinding my pussy against where he smiled.

"Mmm, what else?" he asked, lips smacking together against my clit.

"You fuckin' me."

"Fuckin' you until you cum all on my dick?"

"Yes!" I screamed.

"Mmm, tell me you gon' squirt all over this dick when I give it to you."

"Oh my God, Mav…," I whispered, mouth fixated into an O shape. I buried my face in the nearest pillow and pulled his sheets into my grasp. "Ooooh fuck, I'm cumming!"

"That's a good girl," he said before officially prying his lips away from mine.

I collapsed onto the bed, panting as my body shook. I flipped over and looked at him standing on the side of the bed with his dick in hand. My eyes lit up in delight. He had the juiciest dick I'd ever seen in real life.

"You see what you did? Look how hard this dick is for you, River. Nice and thick for you," he said, stroking his dick. "I'ma give this pussy the pounding it deserves. You ready for it?"

I nodded, trying hard to contain my excitement before flipping back over onto all fours. Mav ran his hands down the back of my thighs before slapping his palm against my ass. He folded my arms across my back and galloped into me, delivering back shot after back shot.

"Mmm! I feel every fuckin' inch!" I screamed, knees sinking deeper into the mattress.

The repeated smacking sound of his thighs against my ass filled the room. He reached around and placed my hand on my clit. "Play with that fuckin' pussy for me," he commanded.

I turned my head back to kiss him. "I'm about to fuckin' cum again," I mumbled against his lips.

He crisscrossed his hands over the small of my back and tossed his dick inside me with quick, deep thrusts.

"Yessss! Yessss! Just like that! Oh my fuckin'—

Ooooh fuck, baby!"

My mouth hung wide open as he pulled my hair, riding me fast and hard. I knew everything I was saying was practically inaudible if they were even real words at all. He had me speaking in tongues. With all the screaming and moaning I was doing, I was thankful his bedroom was on the main floor away from all the other bedrooms in the house.

"Mmm, shit. That pussy wet as fuck for me. Put that pretty ass pussy on my face again. I wanna watch you cum all over my tongue."

Mav gripped my ankles and slid me across the bed before pulling my pussy towards him in a standing sixty-nine position. Suspended upside down in the air, I let my tongue slide up and down the length of his dick. I wrapped both hands around his dick and enveloped the head in between my lips. He thrusted his hips forward as I whipped my head back and forth, trying my best not to gag too hard on his dick. Mav spit inside my pussy while rubbing my clit with his thumb. The slurping of his lips made beautiful music with my moans as he tongue fucked me to my next climax.

MAV PULLED ME on top of him, and I began to rock back and forth against his curved snake. My nails sliced at his chest as he started thrusting into me. He gripped my waist tight while I slipped up and down his pole.

"Ohhhh fuck, I think I'm gonna—oh shit!" I squealed as my fingertips searched for something to dig into. His headboard was so high, I could barely reach the top.

"Yeah, that's right, squirt all over this dick," he said, before leaning forward to suck on my nipples.

He flipped me over on my back and pushed my legs over my head, curling me up like a pretzel. His soft lips kissed down the back of my thighs before parting my legs like the Red Sea and sinking his long tongue deep inside me.

My body curved into a C-shape, flexing my abs. "Oooh sh—shit." I trembled.

"Not yet, baby girl. Not yet. I want you to cream all over this dick again."

It was clear he was a pleaser in the bedroom. I was just trying to keep up. He climbed on top of me and pushed inside me. His key fit my lock to perfection as if we were carved for each other. He pushed in deep and let it press against my g-spot, triggering a wave of shakes throughout my body.

"M—Mav," I whispered.

With my hair spread wildly across the sheets and my ankles at his neck, he massaged and kissed the soles of my feet. My breasts jiggled freely as his dick delivered merciless strokes.

"Tell me when you're about to cum," he insisted.

I sunk my teeth into my bottom lip and locked my knees. Gyrating as hard as I could against him, I flew into my next orgasmic quake.

"Ahh! Yess. R—right Now! I'm cumming right now!" I said, eyes slammed shut.

"Mmm, shit. You look so beautiful when you cum on this dick," he whispered in my ear.

I pulled his lips onto mine as my warm hands cradled the sides of his face. He slowed his stroke to a slow, rhythmic pace. Each deep stroke fused us closer together like magnets. With his chest pressed against me, I could feel his chest rising and falling with rapid breaths. We kissed passionately, trading turns letting our tongues swirl around in the other's mouth. He pulled all the way out to the tip and began slowly feeding me the dick, inch by inch.

"Every. fuckin. inch inside that pussy," he mumbled, keeping a steady rhythm.

"Ahhhh yes!" I shivered, eyes making their way to the back of my head.

156

My nails dug into his shoulder blades, tearing into his flesh like a lion into prey. He was digging out every square inch of my pussy. I locked my arms around his neck as he hovered over me, keeping his breaths steady. When his strokes began to quicken again, he locked his hands underneath my knees. I pressed the soles of my feet into his chest as he bit down on his bottom lip.

"Mmm, fuck," he groaned, tossing his head toward the ceiling. He sucked in air through his teeth before gripping my waist tight and releasing himself. His broad chest pumped rapidly before he looked down at me and slowly pulled away from me.

He turned away and sat on the edge of the bed while shaking his head. "You see what you do to me, River? This can't happen again."

IT HAD BEEN THREE DAYS since Mav and I had taken things to the point of no return, and things had quickly soured. He'd suddenly become more callous than usual and hadn't bothered to touch me or look my way for more than a few seconds at a time. He spent most of his time at his shop. There was a time when I thought I'd broken down the door to his heart, only to be met with another wall with barbed wiring. I didn't understand how he could go from being so passionate and tender with my body as if we were fused together to treating me as if we were on two different sides of the world. Mav was heaven

157

to my body but hell to my heart.

"Auntie River, look at my picture!" Noemi squealed, jarring me out of my thoughts. She raced to my side and shoved her latest creation in my hands.

"Oooh, how pretty! Tell me what it is."

"We are superheroes. That's you, and me, and Uncle Mav."

"Oooh, so cool! What superpower do I have?"

"You can fly really fast, and Uncle Mav is super strong like this!" she said, pumping up her arms to show her muscles.

"And what about you? What superpower do you have?"

"I can close my eyes and see Mommy and Daddy whenever I want."

My eyes instantly welled up with tears. "That's really um, great. I uh, let's put it up on the fridge. How would you like that?"

"Yeah!" she squealed.

I found myself staring at the picture for minutes at a time, only breaking out of my thoughts when I heard the front door open. I walked out of the kitchen to see Mav walking in.

"Hey…"

He nodded. "Sup?"

The moment had presented itself. I had his undivided attention, and Noemi wasn't around to interrupt. *Ask the question, River. Just open your mouth and let the shit fall right out,* I coached myself.

"What's up with you?"

"What do you mean?" he questioned.

I huffed. "There you go, answering my question with a question again. You've been acting distant ever since what went down, and I'm confused. I thought we were on the same page."

"And what page is that?" he interjected.

I sucked my teeth. It wasn't hard to see that his heart was cold and closed tight like a fist and his patience was wearing thin. I just needed to get straight to the point. "What is this between us? Just tell me the truth. It won't hurt my feelings."

Mav

She didn't know how incorrect she was. She couldn't take it. She wasn't ready for me to dead any hope she had of us being anything or take a razor blade to her heart strings. I was still upset with myself for being weak and acting on my impulses. I'd learned a long time ago to control my weaknesses before my enemies could expose them and use them to their advantage. But when it came to River, I just had to have her. After all, it's always the most forbidden fruit that taste the sweetest. She was more to me than just a piece of pussy in a moment of weakness, but I would never tell her she was my kryptonite.

I didn't have time to deal with her feelings when there was so much uncertainty in the streets around Luca's death. I knew I needed to be focused and ready when someone tried to make a move. If that meant I had to choose between my legacy and my heart, then my legacy would win every time. Being in survival mode required me to go back to my primitive way of thinking—having a heart on ice was the only way to be a successful in life. I couldn't surrender my heart to her. It was just easier to cut things where they were before either of us fell any harder. I knew losing her interest could be dangerous, but it was a risk I would have to take at least until things settled down.

"Was it not what you thought it would be? Was your attraction to me just on some only for the night shit?" she quizzed, demanding a response.

160

"That's not it. Far from it."

"Then what is it? I can't be the only one that feels the chemistry between us, right?"

"Chemistry is more than just anatomy. Never confuse the two," I told her.

"And I know that, but I just thought we—"

"Look, I can't do this playing house shit. It's never been my style and it never will be."

"But you're different when you're with me."

"And that's the fuckin' problem, River. I'm no good for you."

"Let me be the one to decide that for myself."

"Ain't shit to decide. From here on out, it's all about Noemi between us. That's it."

She frowned. "So we're not even going to attempt to be friends? I at least thought we were mature enough to do that."

"If you want a friend, get a dog."

She shivered, speechless. My words were bone chilling, like stepping out of the shower and realizing you forgot your towel, chilling. I turned away, sliding her heart in my back pocket and going on about my business.

One month later.

Mav

River and I hadn't uttered more than a handful of words to each other in person in over a month. We only communicated through text, and only when it was something about Noemi. I took the time to myself to put all of my effort into getting my shop open and ready for business and recruiting the best tattoo artists in the city. I walked in the house to see Noemi sitting crisscrossed in the middle of the kitchen floor surrounded by a rainbow of crayons and markers.

"What are you drawing?" I asked before reaching in the fridge to pull out a bottle of water.

"It's a birthday card for Auntie River."

"Birthday card?"

"Today's her birthday, so that means we gotta eat cake, like lots of it. I—I mean, she really likes cake."

I turned down my brow at her before chuckling. "Yeah, okay. It's her birthday for real though?"

"Yeah. What'd you get her? I promise I won't tell."

A loud crack of laughter rolled up through my chest. "Yeah, right, kid. Your little ass can't hold water."

"Mmhm, watch!" she said, before picking up the cup of juice beside her and holding some in her mouth for a few seconds before swallowing it. "See!"

I rolled my eyes. "Truth be told, I didn't get her nothin'. I didn't know it was her birthday, she didn't say anything."

"We should have a party! And cake! Don't forget the cake! For my birthday, Mommy always got me a really big cake, tall like you!" She pointed while staring up at me.

"Like way up here, huh?"

"Yeah, way up there!"

"Okay, well you need to be my little detective then and go find out what type of cake she likes, and you can plan the biggest party you want for her."

"Yeah?"

"Yup, knock yourself out, Kiddo."

"Yay! I'm on it!" she said, scurrying out of the kitchen.

163

River

It was my twenty-sixth birthday, and I couldn't have cared less. I wasn't in the mood to take birthday selfies, open the curtains, or even crack a real smile. I wanted the day to go by as if birthdays weren't even a thing. The sun would rise and fall behind the curtains, and I had no plans to let a single ray of sun into my room, let alone leave my bed. I was perfectly content just laying across my bed, shamelessly scrolling through Instagram and binge-watching old movies. While sinking deeper into my feelings, I heard a light tapping against my door. Already knowing who my visitor was, I kept my eyes fixated on the door.

"Come in!"

Noemi ran in and jumped on the bed beside me. "What are you doing?" she asked.

"Watching a movie."

"What's it about?"

"Um, it's a really old movie about two high school kids who fall in love over the summer…there's a lot of singing and dancing, too," I said, giving her limited details on the 1970s rom-com/musical mash-up that was *Grease*.

"Oh, sounds kinda boring. But uh, I gotta ask you a few questions," she said, pulling out a notebook and pen

164

from her mini MCM bookbag.

"So um, okay, I'm gonna ask you questions, and you tell me the answer, okay?"

"What is this for, little girl?"

"It's a pretend game, okay?"

I side eyed her for a second and then decided to play along. "Okay, fine. Go."

"Um, what's your favorite color?"

"Purple."

"Okay, she said, digging back inside her bag and pulling out a purple crayon before swirling it around on her paper a few times. "Okay, now um, what's your favorite food?"

"Hmm," I paused. If we were playing pretend, I was going to go big. "My favorite food is lobster, and spaghetti, and peanut butter and marshmallow sandwiches, and..."

"Cake?!" she chimed in.

"Yes, cake!"

"Lots of cake!" she squealed.

"SO MUCH CAKE!" I squealed back. It was the

first time I'd smiled all day.

"Okay, what's your favorite um, thing that you um, want from the store?"

"Oh, it's got to be diamonds, my dear. You see, diamonds are a girl's best friend," I proclaimed before reaching out to tickle her belly and underarms. Noemi squealed and squiggled across my bed, filling my room with giggles. Being around her was the first time I smiled all day.

"Okay, well that's all I needed. I'll leave you alone so you can watch your boring movie."

I rolled my eyes. "Gee, thanks."

AFTER WATCHING CINEMATIC CLASSICS from the eighties like *Sixteen Candles, The Breakfast Club,* and *Do the Right Thing* back-to-back, taking a nap, and then taking a shower, I finally decided it was time to venture out of my room. Demanding food, my growling stomach would no longer let me ignore it. I walked downstairs into the kitchen and flipped on the lights to see Noemi and Mav standing in the middle of the floor with birthday hats on.

"Surprise!" Noemi yelled.

"Wow, what is all this?"

"Happy birthday! Welcome to your birthday party!"

I looked around to see damn near everything Noemi

166

and I had talked about taking up countertop space—
including a large sheet cake with purple roses and 'Happy
Birthday, River' written across it in purple icing. I sucked
my teeth. "You said our conversation was pretend! I didn't
need all of this, but um, thank you though."

"Come on, come open your presents so we can eat
your cake. I forgot to ask your favorite, so I got mine."

"Which is?"

"Chocolate!"

"Well I'll be! That's my favorite too!" I told her,
although I was truly a sucker for red velvet.

"We've been waiting all day for your ass to come
out that room," Mav chimed in.

I extended my arms wide before yawning. "Oh.
Y'all could've knocked or something."

"Nah, I told her not to bother you. I figured
whenever you got hungry enough you'd find your way."

"And here I am…"

Silence hung between us for a few seconds before he
spoke up again. "Noemi, give you auntie her gifts."

"Here's your cards that I made you. I made three
because I liked them all, and I wanted you to have them,"

she explained.

A warm smile spread across my face. "Thank you so much. They're all beautiful like you."

"Now open Uncle Mav's gift!" she squawked while handing me a Tiffany and Co. signature blue box that I immediately knew had something expensive in it.

"Um, I'm going to take it upstairs and open it later. I'm really hungry right now, and I want some of that cake!"

"YES, CAKE!" she screamed.

After making my plate and satisfying my hunger, I turned my attention to the box sitting beside me on the bed. It was staring me down, begging for me to open it. Five whole minutes passed before I even let my fingers budge. I contemplated giving it back without opening it or tossing it in the trash, but my curiosity got the best of me in the end. I cracked open the box and saw a sparking platinum bracelet filled with diamonds and rubies inside. My mouth almost hit the floor as I pulled it on and slid it over my hand. I extended my arm while slightly turning my wrist to watch it sparkle from all possible angles.

"It's so beautiful," I whispered to no one but myself.

I quickly searched the small hang tag for a price and sucked in a quick breath when I saw the price. He'd gone out and dropped almost sixty thousand dollars in A DAY on a bracelet. That was more than I made in an entire year! I'd never owned anything that nice before. It was a true statement piece. As in love with it as I was, I knew I couldn't accept it. What did such an expensive gift even mean? Was I supposed to look at it as just an ordinary gift or something more? A long, sad sigh escaped past my lips before I returned the bracelet back to the box. I walked back downstairs to find Maverick and found him out in the garage working out.

"Uh, hey…" I mumbled over the loud music.

He took out his phone to pause Meek Mill. "Sup?"

"I just came down to say thank you for the surprise party and the gift. It's really beautiful, but I can't accept it," I said, handing the box to him.

"Anybody ever told you givin' a gift back is disrespectful?"

"Return it or save it for Noemi to wear one day, I don't care," I said, trying to hand him the box again.

"If I wanted Noemi to have it, I would've bought her one, too."

"You're making this harder than it needs to be…"

"Nah, that's all you. The gift was just somethin' slight for your birthday. It's not a big deal."

169

"If it's not a big deal, then why can't you just take it back?" I quizzed.

"Because I wanted you to have it. I already told you, red looks good on you."

My eyes cascaded down to the fuzzy socks on my feet. "I remember…"

"Look, um, I'm sorry, aight? You know, for being cold to you for all this time," he continued.

I scrunched up my lips. "Thanks, but uh, I don't want your apology. This was nice and all, but it wasn't necessary, so please just take it back," I said, placing the box on his workout bench and walking back inside the house.

I was emotionally seasick from all the back and forth with Mav. First, he breaks me off with some of the best pipe I'd ever experienced, then he tells me we'll never be nothing, only to give me a gift that I confirmed cost well over what I made in an entire year. I could barely look his way without hearing the lyrics to Vivian Green's *Emotional Rollercoaster,* playing in my head. He was hot one day and then ice cold the next, and I was seriously ready to exit the ride for good.

TEN

One month later.

River

Summer break was officially over, and I was preparing to welcome students back to school. I was sitting crisscross in the middle of my desk cutting out decorations for my bulletin board when my phone rang. I glanced down to see "The Devil" on my screen. My eyes bulged and my palms instantly sprang a leak. Leander was calling. Stunned, I hesitated to answer.

I don't need him. My life is perfectly fine without him. He needs to see that he didn't break me! Bitch, I'm back and I'm better! I coached myself before pressing accept. I cleared my throat. "Hello?"

"Hello? River. It's me…Leander. Before you hang up, please just give me thirty seconds of your time to explain myself."

171

I contested. "Ten."

"Okay, okay. First let me say thank you for even answering my call after how I handled things..."

"Five," I said, slicing off the end of his sentence.

"Okay, I'm in town, and I want to see you. To apologize and to explain everything to you in person. You deserve so much more than that, but if you'll have me, I'd really like to see you."

My forehead creased. As long winded as I thought I'd be whenever I did finally hear from his ass, I had absolutely nothing to say in the moment.

"H—hello? River, are you still there?"

"I'm here."

"So, dinner tonight?" he posed.

"Where?"

"Anywhere, you choose."

"I haven't said yes yet," I reminded him.

"Whenever you do decide, let me know and I'll meet you whenever, wherever."

I rolled my eyes. He was not going to woo me that

easily. Yes, there were still feelings there that I hadn't fully dealt with, but as much as I didn't want to give him the pleasure of seeing my face ever again, my ears were burning to know his truth.

"I'll think about it," I replied and hung up.

A FEW HOURS LATER, I found myself standing in the middle of my closet with nothing but my bra and panties on. If I was going to show face, I was going to be snatched from top to bottom. I pulled out two different outfits and walked back out to toss them across the bed. My fingertips whipped up a quick text to Leander with the address to my favorite restaurant.

Me: [6:22pm]: "It's reservation only, so…good luck."

I glanced down at the time. It was 6:17 p.m. I highly doubted he would be able to get reservations on such short notice, but I was glad to get the chance to make him sweat.

Not even thirty minutes later, my phone pinged with Leander's response. *"We're on at 8:45 tonight."*

My heart began to race. There was no way. Absolutely no fuckin' way. I started to text and then quickly erased my message. Fuck. The nerves began to set in, and I'd gone from being Beyonce fierce to a timid school girl. After a few minutes of waiting for my response, Leander called.

"Yeah," I answered.

"I know you saw my text. Why you ain't hit me back yet?"

"I figured you were lying, so…"

"Nah, no bullshit, I got the reservations. My boy's shawty works at the front desk, he got her to move some things around and we in there."

"It was that easy, huh?" I asked with a sarcasm laced in my tone.

"I gotta do what I gotta do to make a good impression. I know that I—you know what, I'll save it for dinner. 8:45, aight? You not gon' make me eat alone are you?"

I chewed my bottom lip trying so hard not to smile. *Goddammit!* I screamed inside my head. Soon, butterflies began to invade my stomach. *Fuccccckkkkkkkk*

"River?"

"8:45, got it," I said and quickly ended the call.

I darted back into my closet and rubbed my clammy hands down my thighs. "What to wear? What to wear?" I mumbled.

All I could hear was Suki's voice in my head tellin'

me all the things I needed to change about myself to get noticed. Maybe that was one of the reasons why Leander left—maybe I was too chill or too boring for his taste. The more I pondered, the more conspiracies I hatched as to why he did me the way that he did.

"Fuck it, I'ma be River 2.0 tonight. I'm gon' show this man every inch of what he left behind and make him eat his fuckin' heart out!" I hissed.

I pulled out the shortest and most revealing thing I owned and threw it on, wet my long curls and tossed in a little leave in conditioner to keep the frizz at a minimum, did my makeup and was ready to go. As soon as my heels clicked against the bottom step, I saw Mav coming around the corner.

He turned up his nose when he saw me. "Where you goin' dressed like that?"

"Out. Why do you care? I'm grown, and I can dress however I want!"

He scoffed and brushed me off. "Yeah, aight, whatever."

"Yeah, whatever."

"I'm sayin' though, don't wear that," Mav said, his voice cutting like a shard of glass against my feelings.

175

My arms quicky flew across my chest. "Excuse me?"

He studied me with piercing scrutiny. "You makin' it too easy for him."

"What makes you think I'm going to meet with a man?"

"Fine—you're makin' it too easy for any nigga. Make 'em work for it."

My brows knitted. "How?"

"You givin' too much away. It's taking away from the best thing about you."

"And what's that?" I asked, fully ready to argue him out of his socks.

"Your face, River."

I stopped dead in my tracks, first looking at the ground, then letting my gaze drift up to his eyes—his judging, unforgiving eyes. My brain fizzled as goosebumps clothed my exposed skin. "Oh."

"I'm just tryna put you on game," he said before turning to leave me with my disoriented thoughts.

I caught an embarrassing glance at myself in the mirror and quickly turned away. He was right. Wearing that dress made it painfully clear that I had gotten too deep into my head and was clearly trying to overcompensate for my nerves. The truth was, I was not okay. There I was, less than an hour away from knowing the truth to the answers that plagued me for months as I tried to mend the heart that he broke. Then, to turn my feelings over to Mav and have him step all over them, yet still feel the need to warn me before I stepped outside the house lookin' like anything but myself.

Mav had made it clear he was the last of a dying breed. He didn't sugarcoat shit. I'd never met another like him, and I probably never would. Before turning to go back upstairs, I whipped out my phone to text Leander.

Me: [8:15pm]: Coming, but I'm going to be a little late.

I ARRIVED AT THE RESTAURANT twenty-two minutes late and saw Leander seated at a table for two a few feet away from the bar. "Leander…" I said, announcing my presence.

He turned his attention to me and looked me up and down before smiling from ear to ear. "River, wow. You look…you're breathtaking."

"Thanks…" I nodded, glancing down at my attire, which consisted of a blazer, tank, wide-legged palazzo pants that made my ass look great, and heels. I felt more like myself and was a lot more comfortable. I took my seat.

"Can I order you a drink?"

"Cosmo," I said, determined to keep it cute. He'd already met emotionally wrecked River on his voicemail, he didn't need to follow up with an introduction to pissy drunk and still pretty emotionally wrecked River that night.

"Well, I know the reason you're probably here is to

hear me explain, so I just—" he paused while reaching out to grab my hand.

I quickly pulled my hand away.

"I'm sorry," he said.

"Just say what you have to say, Leander."

"River, I'm so sorry. I know I handled everything wrong. More than wrong—I handled things like a fuck boy, and you didn't deserve to have to deal with any of that."

"You're right, I didn't," I retorted, "it wasn't as if you breaking up with me through text and then blocking me wasn't bad enough, but then I got surprised with an eviction notice and subsequently thrown out on my ass all because you had me thinking you were handling the bills. How could you leave me holding the bag like that? Did I not mean anything to you? Did what we have not mean anything?"

"You did, and you still do. I had a lot of shit I was dealing with internally and not sharing with you. I'd lost my job six months before I left you, River," he admitted.

"W—what?"

"And I just—my pride just wouldn't let me tell you, so I thought I was gon' be okay for maybe a month and I would have something else lined up in no time, but I couldn't get an interview with anyone. I was going fuckin' crazy, River. It was eating me up lying to you like that every day. It wasn't until I broke down and reached out to my dad that he hooked me up with a job at a firm his frat brother works at. It's great. I've got better benefits, and I'm making fifteen thousand more dollars a year than I was out here."

"I mean, that's good for you, but why did you feel like you couldn't tell me that? Was I so bad of a girlfriend that you felt that I'd emasculate you or something?"

"No, none of that. I'm telling you, River. It wasn't you, it was all me. I was too wrapped up in my head. I was used to being the man of the house, and I went from bringing in money to nothin' but straight rejection after rejection. I was depressed and at that time, I just felt like it would've made me more depressed if you knew what was going on with me because I knew how heavy the load was that I was carrying, and I didn't want that for you."

"But we weren't just some fling. We were in a committed relationship, Leander. For years! I just—I just don't get it. I mean, I guess I get it, I just don't feel like, ugh, I don't know." I huffed as my emotions began to get the best of me.

"Tell me how you feel. I can take it," he assured me.

"Are you sure you're ready for that?"

"Trust me, I know you're one to say how you feel."

179

"I mean, I practically let all of my emotions play out on your voicemail. I really hope you deleted those, by the way," I said, taking a few sips of my drink.

"Nah, I actually still listen to them from time to time when I'm really in need of a self-esteem boost." He chuckled, which made me laugh.

"Shut up. That's not funny. I'm supposed to be lighting into you right now!"

"I'm just tryna lighten the mood here, that's all."

I huffed. "All jokes aside, you really hurt me, Leander. I've never felt pain like that from someone, and then having to deal with that and then losing my best friend and not having you to turn to about it or not having that shoulder to cry on, that was a lot for me. I just—I mean, I appreciate your apology and you finally being man enough to tell me the truth, but it does lead me to wonder where is all of this coming from all of a sudden? You left so abruptly and then you blocked me as if I did something to you, and now you're here basically kissing the ground I walk on. I'm sorry, but this is a lot for me."

"I know, and I respect that. I'm just—you just. I know, I fucked up. I know it will take you a long time to get over what I did to you."

"What is it that you want, Leander? You talked about us meeting like you wanted closure. Yet, you've apologized, and I'm still not understanding why you're still talking."

"You're not going to make this easy for me, are you?"

"Why should I?"

"You shouldn't, and I respect that. I'm here now, and I'm ready to take care of you—to take care of us, if you'll allow me."

"Leander, stop."

"Listen, River. You're all I can think about, all I've been thinking about."

I shook my head. "I don't even know why I'm still here. I got what I came for."

"Maybe you're still here because behind that wall you put up, you still feel something for me."

I sucked my teeth. "I mean, duh, I feel something for you. I feel a lot of things for you and trust me, the majority of them aren't pleasant. But if you're asking if I still love you, I—I don't know if I can give you the answer to that right now."

"Is that because you're scared?"

"It's because I'm not sure. I'm not sure about

anything anymore," I admitted. Unbeknownst to him, he wasn't the only man with access to my heart.

"You're a sure thing, River. And I know that now, and I should've been man enough to tell you how I was feeling when I was feeling it instead of letting it all bubble up and explode the way that it did for us."

"You talk a good game, but if I ever did in a million years decide to give you even the mere piece of a chance, remember that actions speak louder than words."

"How's this for action?" he asked, pulling a velvet ring box out of his jacket pocket and placing it in the center of the table.

My eyes widened. "Leander, what the hell is that?"

"Open it and see."

I shook my head. "No, I want you to tell me what's in that box."

"What's in that box is a second chance, River. The time I spent away made me realize more than ever that I love you, I'm in love with you, and I don't want to lose you."

I slowly cracked open the velvet box and saw a beautiful white gold engagement ring with a moderate-sized solitaire diamond in the center. I could tell he'd spent some real money on it. It didn't hold a candle to the bracelet Mav had gotten me, but it was still nice, nonetheless.

"And what happens the next time you lose a job? How can I be sure that you won't up and leave me again?" I asked, closing the box.

"I've atoned for my sins against you and our relationship, River. I'm asking you for a second chance as your man, and I'm asking you to become my wife..."

My heart raced. "Leander, I...I don't know what to say. This is...this is so fuckin' much. Are you—are you serious?"

He bobbed his head. "I am."

"Wow—this is. I—" I stammered, unable to string together the words to make a proper sentence.

"Take the ring and think about it. I'll be here for two more days. I'm staying at The W downtown. Room 303. If I wake up in two days and the ring is outside of my door, then I'll respect that. But if in two days it's your standing at my door wearing my ring, I promise you I'll never, ever break your heart again."

The air was so thin, I could barely breathe. Every word he spoke seemed to take my breath away. My head was spinning, and I could feel the alcohol churning in my stomach, ready to explode out of my mouth like a volcano at any given moment.

I opened my mouth to speak, but only drew in a limited amount of air. "O—okay," I breathed.

Mav

I was heading down the hallway to my bedroom when I heard River's heels clicking against the entryway floor. I stood back and watched her lug her body into the living room and flop down on the couch. She leaned forward and put something in front of her on the coffee table.

"Late night for you," I commented, coming around the corner.

"I know," she responded, not even bothering to drag her eyes in my direction.

"What's that?"

"An engagement ring…from my ex."

"So, that's where you were?"

"Yup…"

"Damn, that fool asked you to marry him?"

"Fool?"

"Yeah, fool. That nigga is a straight up fool."

She put her mad face on, glaring at me with rage in her eyes. "Is he a fool for wanting to marry me?"

"He's a fool for wanting to get married, period. If he had any sense, he'd know never to get married. A man is a carnal being. We crave more than one person for the rest of our lives. We love our freedom yet insist on locking a bitch down to serve our own selfish desires because no matter how much we love to be free, we can't help but be territorial creatures who will fight to the death over pussy that we won't even respect."

She grimaced. "That's all you have to say?"

"What else was I supposed to say?"

"Nothing, just nothing. Goodnight!" she said, closing the box and brushing my shoulder as she passed me.

Seeing River with an engagement ring in her hand stung a bit. I had to keep treating her as if she was nothing but another lamb to the slaughter in my bed when she was clearly my Achilles heel. River was the bullet and the gun, together we were a deadly pair. My actions had sent her spiraling back to her bum ass ex. I wanted to believe she

185

knew better than to go back to the nigga that played her, but I guess going back to something she was familiar with was better than letting me cut and run with her heart.

ELEVEN

River

    I spent the next day and a half going through the motions; running plays of all the highs and lows of my relationship with Leander through my head and ignoring Mav's existence. I did love Leander and one point in time, and it did make me feel good to be chased and wanted. I still couldn't deny that Mav had caught more than my attention. but he'd made it clear he'd never settle down. He was incapable of loving anyone more than himself, and I couldn't attach myself to a man like that or the hope that he'd change. I had to face the fact that we weren't meant to be.

    "It's been a whole day, and you still ain't speaking to a nigga?" Mav asked, stepping into my space.

    "What is it that you want me to say?"

    "Whatever is on your mind."

187

"Nah, I'm good," I declined.

"I see you wearing that lil' ass ring. You said yes to that fool?"

"I haven't given him an answer yet."

"What you waitin' on?"

I scoffed. "You are unbelievable, you know that? Hot and cold, back and forth. Everything is a game to you, Mav, and I for one am exhausted. One minute you're sweet and vulnerable and the next you're as cold as ice, and I hate even having to be around you! Do you even know who you are? You think you know so much about love and why men do this and do that, and the truth is, you're just as much of a mess as everyone else! You don't have shit figured out about love because you won't allow yourself to be loved! And because of that I don't know how the fuck you're ever going to raise that little girl upstairs on your own!"

"On my own? What the fuck do you mean on my own?"

I huffed. "If I say yes to him, I'd be moving back to Chicago with him, Mav. I wouldn't be living here anymore..."

I watched his face sour. "Well, it seems like you made your choice, so congratulations," he said before turning to walk away.

My heart sank to my feet. I didn't know if I was ready to put so many miles between Noemi and I, but I knew I needed to distance myself from Mav. The two of us were like oil and water; we just didn't mix. The longer I stayed, the more toxic our environment would become.

I PULLED UP to Leander's hotel and wrapped my hands tightly around the steering wheel. I couldn't tear my eyes away from the ring dazzling on my finger. It was enamored with the way it sparkled underneath the streetlights. If love was what I really wanted, and Leander was the man willing to give it to me, I owed him a second chance to prove himself. My feet led me from the car to his hotel room door. My heart thudded in my chest as I reached out to knock.

Leander came to the door a few seconds later and saw the ring box sitting at his feet. He stepped and looked to his right to see me standing there with the ring on my finger.

He smiled wide. "Are you saying what I think you're saying?"

I returned his warm gaze and smiled. "Yes, Leander. I'll marry you, but—"

"Damn, there's a but, baby?" he asked, scooping me in his arms.

"Yes, there's a but. I won't be able to move to Chicago until after the court hearing for Noemi."

189

"Hold up, court hearing?"

"You remember I told you about all of the Noemi stuff? Well, I'm staying with her and her uncle, but it's strictly for Noemi. I'm his one and only character witness, and I have to see this through. Can you respect that?"

"As long as no feelings are involved, then yeah, I trust you. But you have to promise me something in return."

"What?"

"I don't want a long engagement, River. I want you to be mine, so after the court hearing, I want you to become my wife."

"Whoa. That's like a month away, Leander."

"I know it sounds crazy, and it doesn't have to be anything big, it can just be you, me, and our immediate family, okay?"

I sat and thought about his offer for a second and found myself nodding before the words came out of my mouth. If he was going to give me the space I needed to wrap things up in Atlanta with court, my job, and everything in between, then I could get behind the idea of a quick, intimate wedding. Big, showy ceremonies were never really my thing anyway.

LATER THAT NIGHT, I knocked on Noemi's door, equally nervous and eager to share my news with her.

"Look what I've got," I said, showing her the diamond on my finger.

She grinned. "It's pretty! That's a ring like Mommy had."

"Yeah, and you know what that means?"

"What?"

"I'm going to be married like your mom and dad were married."

"You're going to marry Uncle Mav?"

"No! Why would you think that?"

"I like you two here with me."

I shifted my eyes over to her stuffed animals. "So, I do have something else to tell you, and it's not the best news...so, um when I get married, I'll be living with my husband in a new state, and I won't see you every day, but I'll come visit you as often as I can," I assured her.

"Where are you going?"

"Chicago."

"How far away is that?"

"Only a plane ride away. By the time you start watching *Frozen*, you'll be to me."

"Can Uncle Mav, and I come live with you?"

"No, you and Uncle Mav have to stay here in Atlanta, but I'll Facetime you every day!"

"It won't be the same."

"I know you're sad, and I'm sad too, but I promise it'll all be okay."

"I just don't want you to leave me like Mommy and Daddy did."

Tears welled in the back of my eyes. "I'll never—"

"Time for bed," Maverick said, standing in the doorframe.

I turned to look back at him with tears in my eyes.

"Is Uncle Mav going to leave me too?" Noemi asked, shifting my attention back to her.

"I ain't goin' nowhere, Kiddo," he assured her.

"Just remember, I'm always here if you need me."

"Maybe if you marry him, you won't have to leave either of us," Noemi suggested.

"Take your lil' clever butt to sleep and tell your auntie goodnight," he replied to her before I could evenly fully grasp what she'd said.

"Goodnight," she said, lowering her eyes.

"Goodnight, baby girl." I kissed her forehead and climbed out of her bed with tears streaming down my heated red cheeks. I brushed past Maverick and bolted to my room and slammed the door. After flinging myself across my bed, the tears flowed freely, skydiving down to my comforter.

Seconds passed before I heard a gentle knock on the door. I turned my head to see Maverick leaning against the doorframe. "Yo, you aight?"

I turned to face him in all of my shame as if to ask, *Do I look aight?* He stepped in to close the door behind him and slowly started making his way to my bedside. "She's a kid, River. She'll get over it."

"She might, but I won't."

"This is a consequence based off the choice you made."

"I thought you came in here to check on me, not make me feel worse."

"It's the truth."

"What other choice did I have? It's not like you want

193

me." I immediately cringed at myself for letting that last sentence slip past my lips.

"So, that's what this is about? Me not wanting you?" he asked.

I shook my head in protest. I wasn't down to participate in round two of our blowout from earlier. I was too emotionally spent. "Forget I said anything and just close the door behind you," I told him.

"Nah, you said what you said. Just know that none of this shit is about me, aight. Your emotional ass is sittin' in here boo-hoo cryin' for what?"

"I didn't mean to say what I said, so just let it the fuck go."

"But you said it, so what's up?"

I huffed. He was really going to push me over the edge. "All I was saying is that maybe if things had worked out differently for us then things would be different for Noemi, but it's not important anymore. I'm engaged to someone else, and it just is what it is."

"What the fuck you want a nigga to do, huh? Chase you down the aisle? Kill the nigga and proclaim my love for you so we can be a fuckin' family? Get it through your head, River. This ain't what this is, and I been told you that."

"You're right. You're completely right. It's crystal clear that you will only ever care about yourself and there's no room for me in your world. You've created this façade that you don't need anyone but yourself and that might be true because you've made it painfully clear time and time again that you don't need me! So, this is what's best! This ain't no homie, lover, friend shit. We ain't shit! I'll do what I gotta do for you in court, but once that's over, I'm out of your life and out of this fuckin' stupid ass city!" I exploded.

Mav didn't bother replying and instead trekked back out into the hallway and slammed my door in his wake. I was nothing but a ticking timebomb of emotion and if something didn't give, I was going to blow.

TWELVE

River

A few days passed and I'd gotten the much-needed time to get my mental back intact. I'd allowed myself to get used to the idea of being engaged and soon becoming someone's wife. Leander was a good man, and I knew if he kept his promises to me, I could allow myself to be happy with the life we would have together. Yet, there was still a small part inside of me that pondered the question *What if,?* buzzing around my heart like an annoying little gnat. Instead of trying to process my feelings and how one-sided they were, I pushed those thoughts aside and went into Noemi's room with a clothes basket filled with freshly washed clothes. In the midst of picking up a few of her scattered toys and shoving her folded clothes back into their drawers, I started to hear a constant vibrating sound. I peered in drawers, underneath her bed, and even her hamper until I found an iPhone buried near the bottom of her toybox.

"What the hell is this?" I quizzed, looking it over.

I decided to investigate later and shoved it in my back pocket to continue with what I was doing. When I got downstairs, Mav was coming through the front door. Our last conversation had gone awry, and as much as I wasn't in the mood to have a conversation turn into a fight, I wanted to show him the phone. "I found this mixed in with Noemi's toys."

"What's that?"

"A real phone."

"She had a phone? Does it work?"

"I don't know whose it is. I just heard vibrating over and over. At first, I thought I was trippin', but then boom, here's a whole phone."

He shrugged. "Maybe it's a play phone or something. Let's just ask her."

I followed behind Mav as we walked into the living room where Noemi was. "Hey, Noemi, is this yours?" I asked.

She shook her head. "No, that's Mommy's phone," she said nonchalantly.

"Your mommy gave it to you? It was mixed in with your play stuff."

"It was Mommy's secret phone," she whispered.

"Secret phone?"

"Yeah, she told me it was our little secret, so I kept it safe in my toybox."

"Got it, thanks," I said, walking out of earshot. "Did you hear that?" I asked Mav as we stepped around the corner.

"Yeah, a secret fuckin' phone? I knew somethin' wasn't right!"

I rolled my eyes. "It's just a phone. You're talking like it's a Blue's Clue or something."

"It's a secret, and where there's a secret, there's a lie."

"Let's just try and unlock it before you jump off the deep end with conspiracies," I said, first trying Noemi's birthday as the unlock code. The screen shook, telling me I was incorrect.

"All I'm saying is I knew this shit was fishy from the beginning. Fishy as fuck!"

"Give me some other dates. Birthdays, anniversaries…something."

"I don't know, but if you keep typing in the wrong

198

code then—"

"Oops," I muttered, "it's disabled now."

He groaned. "I got somebody who can unlock it, just may take him a bit."

"Who?"

"Don't worry about that, just give me the phone, and I'll take it from here."

Mav

THE WEEKEND ROLLED around once more, and I was eager than a mothafucka. My tattoo shop, M3, was officially opening. I stepped out of my room, drippin' in diamonds and gold, ready to let all of Atlanta know I still had the city on lock. Since River and I seemed to be on speaking terms again, I decided to extend the olive branch and invite her to my grand opening.

"Yo," I said, stepping in her direction. My eyes traveled from the top of her head down to the overnight bag sitting at her feet. "Where you going?"

"Oh, um I'm going to Chicago for the weekend."

"Word?"

"Yeah, why?"

I ran my hand down the back of my head. "Nah, it's cool. My uh—my grand opening of my shop is tonight. I thought it might be cool for you to slide through and see some of your ideas for the layout come to life."

"Oh, um…yeah, sorry. I can't. I'm actually heading to the airport in a couple of hours. I'm flying to Chicago for the weekend to start hashing things out with the wedding. Things are happening really fast."

"Bet." I nodded, no longer interested in having a conversation about her wedding.

"Yeah, but uh…congratulations though."

"Yeah. Thanks…You gon' be back in time for court on Monday?"

She bobbed her head up and down. "Yeah."

"You sure?"

"Yes, Mav. I haven't forgotten. I'll be there," she assured me.

After the red tape was cut, patrons flooded into M3

to get tatted by some of the dopest artists in the city. Liquor was flowing, ink was running, and dollars were rolling in like ocean waves. I couldn't have asked for a more successful grand opening. M3 was my legacy. It was my dream come true, even. But as much as I wanted to celebrate and really let loose, there were two things killing my vibe: the upcoming court date and not having River by my side on one of the biggest nights of my life. She was the missing piece to my puzzle, and without her, I would probably never feel complete.

IT WAS THE MORNING of my court date, and I'd been in a focused mood ever since my eyes cracked open at dawn. I did my best to try to keep the nerves at bay. There was no room for butterflies and sweaty palms in my life. As much as I hated going to court, I planned to walk away with the final say going in my favor, and I had a good chance with River as my character witness. We hadn't spoken since before she'd left for Chicago. I hated how things had been between us, but I knew there was no one to blame but myself. I had to do what had to be done, and I couldn't let my regrets derail me.

"Nice suit," my lawyer said as he approached me.

He was complementing my custom fitted Armani suit. It was nothing for me to dress the part. Looking professional was a sign of respect for the court. "Thanks."

"Remember, the goal is to get the judge to decide in our favor so that you remain the person Noemi lives with primarily. Now, the grandmother is likely going to try and use your past against you but stay grounded and don't let your temper get the best of you. The judge hears so many of these cases a day, that this shouldn't last long. Just go in there and put your best foot forward."

"I got this." I nodded before I stepped inside the small courtroom.

"Good morning, we're here to discuss the concerns about the ability of a Mr. Maverick Malone to be a fit guardian for the child, correct?" The judge huffed.

It was only fifteen minutes after eight o'clock, and his old ass looked like he hadn't slept in a week. All I could do was pray he actually paid attention and heard me out. I wasn't in the mood to have my plea fall on deaf ears. Each chance I got, I turned my attention to the back of the courtroom and scanned the seats behind me for River. She still hadn't shown up by the time Suki's mother got on the stand.

"Can you speak to your relationship with your granddaughter?"

"Oh, of course! Noemi is my little angel. I was there from the moment she was born, and I haven't missed a beat. I'm there for every birthday party, every holiday, every everything because that's what a good grandma does! She

202

needs to be in a stable environment—not in a house where God knows what happens under that roof!"

"Objection, Your Honor!" my attorney shouted out. "There was a walk through done of Mr. Malone's home and everything was found to be above board and stable. There was absolutely no evidence of anything that pointed to any drug, alcohol, or sexual misconduct inside my client's residence."

The judge turned to Suki's mother. "Do you have any evidence to support your claims of misconduct?"

"I don't need evidence. Look at his rap sheet, it's two miles long! He barely knows Noemi—all someone like him knows is the streets, and I do not want my granddaughter growing up around his chosen...lifestyle when she can have a perfectly stable home with us."

"Mrs. Lawrence, I'll remind you of this only once. This is a court of law. You must have irrefutable evidence to prove what you're talking about. Leave your opinions out of it," the judge hissed.

"Sorry."

"I've heard enough. Mrs. Lawrence, you may step down. Mr. Malone, you may now take the stand."

It took everything in me not to slap that bitch into next week. She was really trying to paint me out to be a monster when the truth was, she didn't know the first thing about me. All she needed to see were my tattoos and hear about my past and her mind was made up about me.

"What do you do for a living?" the judge asked as soon as I took the stand.

"I recently purchased a building and plan to open up my own tattoo shop."

"So, you're an entrepreneur?"

I nodded. "Yes."

"And how long have you been the primary caretaker of the minor?"

"Since her parents died."

"Have you shared any of the responsibility with Mr. and Mrs. Lawrence in that time?"

"No, only River."

"Who?"

"Um, she's also listed as the guardian of the minor's estate in the will, Your Honor," my attorney chimed in.

The judge turned to me. "As you know, Mr. Malone. It is my job to ensure that the court acts in the best interests of the child. Mr. and Mrs. Lawrence can give her a stable home and possibly even moral advantages. What can you give her?"

"Moral advantages? Your Honor, I provide for her financially, so she doesn't have to touch any of the money her parents left her. I put food on the table, and I made arrangements to keep Noemi enrolled in the same school her parents wanted her to go to. If you take her away, she'll be moving out of the city."

"She needs to move! She's not safe there! Ask him about her sprained wrist!" Suki's mother yelled.

"Objection!"

His gavel slammed down. "There will be order in this court, Mrs. Lawrence. Outbursts like that are not allowed and will not be tolerated!"

"I'm sorry, Your Honor."

"Mr. Malone, you may continue."

I grimaced. "All I'm really trying to say is, you don't get to choose your parents, none of us do. I may never live up to the type of father that my brother was to her, but I love having the opportunity to watch her grow every day. Am I perfect? No. Is shit easy every day raising this sassy ass lil' girl? No. But the truth is, I can't imagine my life without her. I'm only asking that you let that continue."

"That was very compelling, Mr. Malone. But please refrain from using swear words in my courtroom from here on out," he scolded.

"I'm sorry, Your Honor."

"You may step down. Are there any others who would care to speak on Mr. Malone's behalf?"

"Uh—" my lawyer paused.

I quickly scanned the courtroom for a familiar face, and all I saw was Suki's mother frowning back at me. River still hadn't shown up. If she missed out on my court date and Suki's parents ended up winning custody, she was going to be fuckin' dead to me.

"Well?" the judge asked.

The courtroom doors swung open and in rushed River with a large gust of wind behind her. "I'm here! I'm here! Your Honor, I'm sorry I'm late. Can I please still testify?" she asked, her chest rising and falling with every breath.

"And you are?"

"River—River Newman."

"Can you testify to your experiences with the child around Mr. Malone?"

"Yes, I can."

"Fine, you may take the stand."

River's eyes caught mine as she took her seat. She

was visibly frazzled, and I was sure I was going to hear the story about it later.

"What is your role in regards to the minor?" the judge quizzed.

"I um, I'm the guardian of her estate, and I am her, uh—co-guardian alongside, Mav. I mean, Mr. Malone."

"And you can attest that the home is stable?"

"Yes, everything really does run like an unconventional, messy, well-oiled machine," she admitted. "He drops her off and picks her up from school every day. I cook dinner, he plays with her. He's always spending time with her. You can see it in his eyes when he looks at her that he loves her like she's his own. Honestly, I can't see another man besides her father doing a better job raising her than he has. He's proven it to me, and out of anyone in this room, I've been one of his biggest critics."

"Thank you, Miss Newman. You may step down now."

The central air hissed through the old vents of the courtroom as everyone waited on pins and needles for the judge to announce his decision.

"After hearing from everyone and reviewing the information provided, I have made my decision. Full custody of the child will remain as the late parents requested in their will, with Mr. Malone as the primary guardian, splitting co-guardianship with Miss Newman. If you wish, another date can be set to discuss grandparent visitation. Court is adjourned."

I WALKED OUTSIDE of the courthouse feeling like nothing could wipe away the smile I was wearing. I'd been grinning from ear to ear for five minutes straight. After I shook my lawyer's hand, I darted over to the nanny, who was sitting with Noemi until court was over, and scooped her into my arms for a hug. River joined us a few minutes later.

"Congratulations, Mav. I'm really happy for you."

"Thanks. For a second, I didn't think you were gonna pull through for a nigga," I admitted.

"I know, and I'm sorry. I was supposed to meet with the caterer and then the appointments got switched at the last minute, so I had to try and change my flight. I caught the earliest flight out of Chicago that I could and then hit so much damn traffic trying to get here. I was so scared I wasn't going to make it, but I'm glad I did."

"Me too. you really came through in the clutch. Now the next step is officially adopting her."

She smiled before leaning down to kiss Noemi goodbye. "I'll see you soon, okay?"

"You leaving already? I thought we might go out to celebrate," I told her.

"Like what? As a family? That's not what we are, right?" she bit back.

I bit my lip. She was souring my mood. "Nah, you right. It'll just be me and Lil' Shawty for the rest of the day," I said, picking her up and kissing her cheek.

"Look, I've got a flight to catch, so I'll see the two of you in three weeks in Chicago for the wedding?"

"Yeah."

"Don't forget, Mav. I really need Noemi to be there. It'll mean so much to me."

I nodded. "I got you."

She turned her eyes back to Noemi. "Goodbye, baby girl. I'll see you in a few weeks. I love you so, so, so much!"

"I love you too."

River turned to walk in the opposite direction, and I called out to her. "Aye, yo River."

"Yeah?" she asked, whipping back around.

"Have a safe flight…"

She sighed. "Goodbye, Mav," she said, biting back tears.

Watching her walk away was the hardest things I'd ever done, but she'd chose her side. I wasn't going to interfere with her decision. I didn't do anything to deserve her, so I was going to be man enough to let another man love her the way I was too stubborn to.

THIRTEEN

Three weeks later.

Mav

    I couldn't believe River was getting married. Even more so, I couldn't believe I'd boarded a plane to make sure I gave her the one thing I knew she wanted most, to have Noemi there on her special day.

    "I really like the sparkles on my dress," Noemi said, picking at her hem.

    "Yeah, it looks nice," I told her.

    "I bet Auntie River has a pretty dress, too."

    I lazily shrugged my shoulder. "Yeah, maybe."

    "Are you coming in with me when we get there?"

    I shook my head. "Nah, I'm good.

"Why not?"

"I got some stuff to do. Besides, I don't think your auntie would want me there anyway."

"Why not?"

"I don't know."

"I don't think that," she told me.

"Oh yeah, and what makes you an expert?" I quizzed.

"She loves you."

"She what?"

"She loves you," she repeated.

"She told you that?"

"No!"

"So, you makin' stuff up now?"

"No! I didn't lie. She loves you and you love her too."

My forehead crumpled. "Where'd you get that idea?"

"From Gammy. She said if you're a Christian you

gotta love everybody all the time."

I rolled my eyes before gripping the steering wheel of the rental car tighter. The closer we got to the church, the more anxious I became. When the GPS let me know we'd arrived, I shot River a quick text to let her know we were outside. Minutes later, she came out with her hair and makeup done wearing an ivory velour jumpsuit. She smiled wide when Noemi let the window down.

"There's my girl! Come here and give me a hug! I missed you! Five Facetime calls a day isn't enough!" she squealed, taking Noemi into her arms.

"Aight, y'all have fun. Just uh, shoot me a text when you want me to come get her, or I'll text you the address of the hotel we're at."

"You're not coming in?" River asked.

"Uh, nah. I um, I got some stuff to handle, phone calls to make, you know, to make sure everything at the shop is running smooth like I want."

River pressed her lips tightly together before nodding. "Oh, yeah. I forgot your shop opened. Congratulations, again…"

"Yeah, thanks." I nodded.

A large pause wedged its way in between us, and I

went ahead and put the car back in drive. I needed to leave. Before I pulled off, I stole one last look at her. "For what it's worth, you do make one beautiful bride."

She nodded and gave a ghost of a smile. "Thank you..."

She turned to walk away with Noemi's hand in hers and I pulled off, stealing glances of them in my rearview. It wasn't like I was from the city, so I didn't have a lot of places to go outside of grabbing something to eat and going back to my hotel room. So, I circled the block and parked in the church parking lot. My mind began to race. River was the first woman to ever look at me and see through me. Although I never saw myself admitting it before, she made me better. I hadn't been able to get her off my mind since the last conversation we had at the courthouse. Watching her walk away that day did something to me. Time apart from her hadn't done me any justice either. It only made me miss her more. Seeing how goddamn beautiful she looked only made me want her more.

I didn't know what to do. On the one hand, I knew I would regret letting her walk away from me again but barging into a church would make me nothing but a fool and a walking contradiction of everything I'd ever talked about and knew to be true when it came to love. But, if a five-year-old could see it, then I knew I hadn't done a good job at covering up my true feelings for River. Was I ready to confess my love for her?

River

I took one last look at myself in the mirror before grabbing my bouquet and heading for the door. I drew in a sharp breath as I tried to relish in my last few moments as a single woman. Soon, River Newman would be no more, and I'd become Mrs. Leander Bennet.

"Well, how do I look?" I asked Noemi, who was holding on tight to her basket filled with rose petals.

"You look beautiful." She smiled.

I beamed. "Thank you."

"Uncle Mav thinks so, too."

"What?"

"I think he's sad."

"Sad? What's he sad about?" I asked, trying to keep up with her thought process.

"I think he misses you like I do," she confessed.

My breath stalled before I forced a smile. "I miss you too."

"What about Uncle Mav? Do you miss him?"

"I—er. It's uh—it's complicated."

"But you love him, right? Like you love me?"

"I could never love anyone more than I love you." I smiled before kissing her forehead. "Now c'mon, let's go get me married."

ONCE THE CEREMONY STARTED, Noemi walked down the aisle, dropping her flowers, then I soon followed with my father on my arm.

"Welcome family, friends, and lovers alike. We are here today to unite Leander and River in marriage. Today, we will all witness two become one," the pastor announced.

Leander and I grabbed hands and smiled at each other. We then turned our attention to the pastor, who was also Leander's father. It meant a lot for him to be able to marry us, and we got to use the church for free.

"Now, before we all bow our heads and go to the Lord in prayer, is there anyone here who can attest as to why these two should not be wed today? Speak now or forever hold your peace."

As expected, the room was silent, making it easy to hear my heart thumping like a drum. My soon to be father-in-law then moved onto the vows. Once Leander said, "I do," he turned his eyes to mine. It was my turn.

"And River, do you take Leander to be your lawfully wedded husband? To have and to hold in sickness and health, good times and bad, for rich or for poor, as long as you both shall live?"

Before my lips could part to answer, the doors opened. "I got somethin' I think I need to say," Mav announced.

I gasped, unable to believe my ears or my eyes. There he was, bursting into my wedding ceremony like the hurricane he was. I suddenly felt like I'd been kicked in the stomach, causing all the air to leave my body. With bulging eyes, I released my grip on Leander's hands. "Mav? Wh— what are you doing?"

"I can't let you go…"

I was clenching my jaw so tightly it hurt. "What?"

"I can't let you marry him."

"What the hell is going on here?" Leander interjected.

"I'm sorry, but I love her too," Mav confessed.

Every muscle in my body stiffened as scarlet heat warmed my cheeks. I was past embarrassed. I was *mortified*. How in the hell was I going to explain anything to Leander's family and my own? My eyes burned with rage as I pierced them into Mav. "Are you out of your mind?" I gritted my teeth as my heart leapt out of my chest with each passing second. I was trying my best not to drop any f-bombs in the house of the Lord.

"I love you."

"Wh—"

"And before you answer, I just need you to hear me out."

Leander turned his attention back to me, a deep frown creasing his brow. "I thought you said no feelings were involved," he said bitterly.

"They're not, I just—let, ugh. Just please give me a moment."

The closer I got to Mav, the faster my brain began to step away from all logic. The moment we stepped outside the church, I lit into him like lightning. "You've got some fuckin' nerve!" I hissed.

"I know I do, but just hear me out."

"What could you possibly say to me right now in this moment? I'm seconds away from becoming someone's wife, Mav! If there was ever a time to say whatever it is you're going to say, it's passed!"

"Right now, in this moment you gotta know that you were right. You were right about everything, and I'm sorry."

"You crashed my wedding to tell me that you're sorry? Have you lost your damn mind?"

"You told me you wanted to be chased, here I am chasing you all the way to Chicago to tell you that I love you, River."

I shook my head in disbelief. "Wow."

"What?"

"You're so mothafuckin' selfish!" I exploded. "Why even tell me now? You weren't getting your way and you had to show off your balls and crash my wedding?"

He parted his lips to confess, "My pride wouldn't let me."

"Well, your pride has terrible timing."

He shrugged before his posture stiffened. "Better late than never, right?"

"No! Sometimes, never late is better, Mav. I'm sorry, but you're too late this time. I don't—no, I *can't* trust you with my heart again."

"Can you trust me to love you the way you deserve to be loved?" he posed.

"I don't understand where any of this is coming from. I mean—it wasn't too long ago that you were making it painfully clear that you didn't want me."

"I never not wanted you," he admitted, "you read

219

me from day one. I never knew love before you and Noemi, and to be honest, I had no intention of ever entertaining the idea, but I met my match in you. So, if it's my heart you want, I'm letting you know right now that you've been had it."

I scoffed. As pretty as his words were, he was mistaken if he thought they'd make me go easy on him. Not only had he broken my heart, but he'd embarrassed the shit out of me on one of the most important days of my life. No. Hell no! He was not getting let off that easy.

"You want to love me when it's convenient for you. When you're ready to stop playing and finally start listening to your feelings I'm just supposed to drop whatever it is that I'm doing and love you back? Is that what you want me to do?" I asked, a twinge of anger laced in my voice.

"I want you to tell me you don't love a nigga, too. If you can do that, I'll let you go forever. You can go back in there, and you can marry some other nigga who will never love you like I can."

"I—"

"Tell me you don't love me, River. I'll take that L if you want me to," he pledged.

"Mav, I—"

"Tell me you don't miss my body pressed against yours. Tell me we don't fit together like a hand in fuckin' glove. Tell me you don't want me to kiss you right now," he said, gently caressing the sides of my face.

"Mav, you talk like everything is simple. This is my wedding day. There's another man right on the other side of that door that wants to make me his wife and here you are telling me everything I wanted to hear, but I just—"

I could feel the wall I'd built crumbling from the top down. A tear rolled down my cheek, and he immediately kissed it away. "Tell me I'm breaking your heart right now, and I'll walk away."

As easy as it should've been for me to tell him to leave, to walk away and never infiltrate my heart or my thoughts again, I knew the damage had already been done. Maverick had unlocked something inside of me that not even Leander had been able to do in all the time we were together. I had to come clean with myself. It was time to stop repressing my feelings and to finally be upfront with what and *who* I really wanted.

"Don't..." I whispered.

"Don't what?"

"Don't stop telling me you love me."

"I love you, River. I love you like a mothafucka," he said, his dark-eyed gazed tugging at my heart strings.

He pressed his lips against mine, holding them there for a few seconds before falling deeper into it. As I knew there were about fifty people inside the church that I owed an answer to, but kissing Mav felt too good to stop.

"Tell me I'm yours and you're mine," he mumbled, lips slowly parting from mine.

I smiled. "Maverick Muhammad Malone, I'm yours, forever."

He was the man I never knew I needed. Together, the three of us made a family, which was something Noemi deserved. I knew he was going to be a great father and couldn't wait to spend a couple of forevers with him.

FOURTEEN

Mav

Having River by my side had me feeling like I was sitting on top of the world. That high was short-lived when I got the word from Tek that he was able to unlock the phone River had found in Noemi's things. After I picked it up, I sat in the parking lot and went through it. Heat raced through my veins as I dug into her call log, contacts, camera roll, voicemails, and email. All of all of my feelings had been bottlenecked up until that point—swelling up and boiling over. I'd been delaying the majority of my grief until I knew the truth, but everything I was seeing did nothing but arouse rage inside me.

There were dozens of messages from unsaved numbers, all listing different price points for different sexual favors. Suki had been tricking with high end ballers, even enemies of my brother and I behind Luca's back. In her camera roll were screenshots of multiple paternity tests that were done around the same time as mine with the names

223

blacked out. Out of all the numbers in her call log, there seemed to be two 803 numbers she frequently corresponded with. I went to her voicemails and listened to the last three that were left before she died.

"You know who it is, bitch. I'm not fuckin' with you no more. Run me my three mill or I'm sending the video of you toppin' me off in the elevator to your nigga. See how long your happy home stays happy after that."

"Oh, you must think I'm playin' wit' yo stupid ass, hoe. Keep fuckin' with a nigga like me, and both you and your nigga gon' end up dead."

"You got twenty-four hours to run me what you owe me, or you gon' pay up with your life."

I quickly scanned all of her texts in search for a video until I found a fifteen-second clip of Suki on her knees in an elevator sucking a nigga's dick. He was standing under the camera and couldn't be identified. All I could see was him throwing a stack of dollar bills at her before stepping off the elevator and her picking them up and scurrying off behind him.

"What the fuck? She had something to do with it from the beginning," I mumbled, teeth clenching angrily against my words.

Finding out that Suki was three million in debt with another nigga and fuckin' around on my brother had my head spinning. It was a hard pill to swallow knowing she'd been the sole reason for my brother's downfall, but what I didn't know was who the other nigga was, and why she owed that amount. I hated Suki's ass with everything in me. If she wasn't already dead, I would've killed that bitch myself. I tossed the phone in the passenger seat and sped home. When I walked in, River was coming down the stairs. "Hey," she said, walking over to kiss my cheek.

"Sup?"

Her lips turned down. "What's wrong?"

"What makes you think something's wrong?"

"I can see it all over your face. You're visibly upset," she confirmed.

I let out an irritated sigh and walked into the kitchen. She followed behind me as I leaned forward, my fingers laced before me on the countertop. "Tek was able to unlock the phone, so I picked it up earlier," I told her.

"Did you go through it?"

"Yeah, I did."

"And? What was on it?"

"See for yourself," I said, pulling it out of my back pocket and handed it to her.

She took the phone. "What exactly am I supposed to be looking at?"

"Proof that their car accident wasn't an accident, River. My brother and Suki were murdered."

Her hands shook as she looked through the phone. "W—what is all of this, Mav? What the fuck was Suki into?"

My lips parted, but before sound could come out, the doorbell rang. I shot my eyes to River and then made my way to the door.

"Maverick Malone?" a white police officer asked.

I grimaced. "Who wants to know?"

"You are under arrest for the murder of Luca and Suki Malone. You have the right to remain silent. Anything you say can and will be used against you in the court of law…"

To Be Continued

a note from k.l. hall.

Reader,

Thank you for reading part one of, *The Illest Taboo*. Please, if you've made it this far, I hope you'll consider taking a minute to tell me what you thought about the book in the form of a **book review and/or rating**. Don't hesitate to let me know what you'd like to see from me next! I thoroughly enjoy reading your reviews and hearing from you as well! I'm always striving to attract new readers and retain current ones, and reviews are one of the easiest ways to attract readers. If you loved the book, tell a friend, and most importantly let me know!

k.l. hall

P.S. I created a special playlist just for this book. Check it out by clicking here. (E-Book Only)

about the author.

As a serial storyteller, K.L. Hall pens enthralling love stories intertwined with the grittiness of urban fiction. Her writing style is a fusion of eminently relatable female characters like Sydney Tate and Raquel Valentine, and the flawed, yet desirable male leads who love them, like Law Calloway and Justice Silva.

Reader Faves:
In the Arms of a Savage: (Peaked at #1 in Women's Fiction)
As Long as You Stay Down: (Peaked at #2 in African American Erotica)
Awakened: A Paranormal Romance: (Peaked at #1 in Erotic Science Fiction)

Sign up for my mailing list to stay up to date with new releases, giveaways, sneak peeks, and more! Click this link: https://bit.ly/38RMpV5 *(E-Book Only)*

Connect with me on social media:

Facebook: K.L. Hall_

Twitter: @authorklhall

Instagram: @authorklhall

Website: www.authorklhall.com

UP NEXT: The Illest Taboo 2

Other novels by K.L. Hall:

Diary of a Hood Princess 1-3

Rise of a Street King: The Justice Silva Story *(Spin-Off to the Diary of a Hood Princess series)*

Where He Belongs: A Disrespectful Love Story

Love Me Harder: A Sin City Love Story

Broken Condoms and Promises 1-3

In the Arms of a Savage 1-3

Built for a Savage: Blaze and Camille's Love Story *(Spin-Off to the In the Arms of a Savage Series)*

A Ruthle$$ Love Story 1-3

Fallin' for the Alpha of the Streets 1-2

The Most Savage of Them All: The Wolfe Calloway Story *(Prequel to the In the Arms of a Savage Series)*

When a Gangsta Loves a Good Girl

Caught Between my Husband and a Hustler

The Illest Taboo

Novellas:

Bi-Curious: An Erotic Tale

House of Cards

A Savage Calloway Christmas *(Christmas novella to the In the Arms of a Savage Series)*

Lovin' the Alpha of the Streets: A Valentine's Day Novella *(Valentine's Day novella to the Fallin' for the Alpha of the Streets Series)*

Awakened: A Paranormal Romance

As Long as You Stay Down

Children's Books:

Princess for Hire

Princess Twinkle Toes & the Missing Magic Sneakers

Little One, Change the World

Adjust Your Crown: A Self-Love Coloring Book for Children of Color

CPSIA information can be obtained
at www.ICGtesting.com
Printed in the USA
LVHW021530250721
693637LV00006B/166